BIONICLE®

Time Trap

BIONICLE®

*FIND THE POWER,
LIVE THE LEGEND*

The legend comes alive in these exciting BIONICLE® books:

BIONICLE Chronicles
#1 Tale of the Toa
#2 Beware the Bohrok
#3 Makuta's Revenge
#4 Tales of the Masks

The Official Guide to BIONICLE

BIONICLE Collector's Sticker Book

BIONICLE Mask of Light

BIONICLE Adventures
#1 Mystery of Metru Nui
#2 Trial by Fire
#3 The Darkness Below
#4 Legends of Metru Nui
#5 Voyage of Fear

#6 Maze of Shadows
#7 Web of the Visorak
#8 Challenge of the Hordika
#9 Web of Shadows

BIONICLE Encyclopedia

BIONICLE®

Time Trap

by Greg Farshtey

SCHOLASTIC INC.
New York Toronto London Auckland Sydney
Mexico City New Delhi Hong Kong Buenos Aires

ISBN 0-439-74559-4

LEGO, the LEGO logo, and BIONICLE
are trademarks of The LEGO Group. © 2005 The LEGO Group.
All rights reserved. Published by Scholastic Inc.
SCHOLASTIC and associated logos are trademarks and/or
registered trademarks of Scholastic Inc.

12 11 10 9 8 7 6 5 4 3 2 1   5 6 7 8 9 10/0

Printed in the U.S.A.
First printing, October 2005

For Michael and Maria, with love

INTRODUCTION

Turaga Vakama stood at the bow of a small boat making its way across the waters to Metru Nui. All around him, the hastily assembled Matoran fleet was cutting through the waves, bearing the former residents back to the City of Legends.

It had been a long, hard journey to reach this point. One thousand years ago, the Toa Metru had succeeded in saving the Matoran from the ruins of this city. They had sacrificed their power and become Turaga to awaken the villagers, and then built a new world on the island of Mata Nui. There they suffered Rahi attacks and other disasters spawned by the evil Makuta, who desired complete control over the Matoran.

Finally, after so many years, six Toa had arrived to defeat Makuta's minions and restore

1

hope to the Matoran. Thanks to their efforts and those of the Toa of Light, Metru Nui had been rediscovered. The Matoran were going home at last.

A great weariness overtook Vakama. He had spent many nights telling the Toa Nuva the tales of Metru Nui. Some had been inspiring stories of heroism against great odds, and some tales filled with fear and regret. Now the heroes were armed with truth as they joined the Matoran on their journey home.

The sight of the Metru Nui skyline, even as badly damaged as it was, should have filled Vakama with only joy and relief. But there was another emotion mixed with those, one harder to define. There were memories here for him that the other Turaga did not share. Another tale had taken place here, one that he had never told his friends or the Toa Nuva.

As the boat drew closer to the shore, Vakama closed his eyes and remembered a day when he and the other Toa Metru were leaving their city far behind.

Toa Matau stared hard at Toa Vakama. The two were almost mask to mask, Matau's eyes boring into his friend's as if Vakama were some previously unknown breed of Rahi beast. After a few moments, Matau broke off and started walking around the Toa of Fire, all the while muttering to himself.

"*What* are you doing?" Vakama demanded finally.

"I always knew you would go crazy one day," Matau replied. "Not Hordika-crazy, just mad-crazy all on your own. I want to remember the sight."

At one time, Vakama would have reacted with anger to Matau's joke. But he had recently learned all too well what happened when one allowed the darker emotions to dominate. Instead, he said quietly, "I'm not crazy. All I said was, I am going back to Metru Nui. The rest of you take the Matoran to the island above, and I will join you soon."

At the controls of the airship in which they flew, Onewa sat shaking his head. They had just finished a terrible struggle to overcome the Visorak horde and escape the city. In the holds of their small armada of ships were a thousand silver spheres, each one containing a Matoran trapped in an endless sleep. It had been a miracle they had made it out of Metru Nui at all, let alone that they managed to save the whole population. And now Vakama wanted to go back!

"After all this time, I know better than to argue with you," Onewa said over his shoulder. "But do you mind telling us why? Did you leave a lightstone on or something? Forget your favorite Kanoka disk? What?"

Vakama gazed out of the cockpit at the dark city below and the silver sea that surrounded it. "Something a little more important than that, Onewa. With all that has happened to us, I'm not surprised it slipped your mind . . . though

4

I would not have thought it easy to forget the Mask of Time."

Those three final words were enough to bring the conversation to an abrupt halt. All of the Toa present remembered how Vakama crafted the Kanohi Vahi, the Mask of Time, with the power to slow down or speed up time around a target. Keeping the powerful mask out of the hands of the evil Makuta had nearly cost Vakama his life, and had led to the death of Turaga Lhikan. During the course of the battle, the Vahi had fallen into the sea.

"It's still down there," said Vakama. "If it should fall into the hands of Makuta, all that we have done here, and all our hopes for a new life, will be erased. I have to find it."

"We'll all go," Nokama said. "If it's that important —"

Vakama shook his head. "You have to get the Matoran to safety. If I am wrong, and Makuta has forgotten the mask, he will go after them. If I am right, then at least I can delay him long enough for you to escape . . . perhaps even to destroy the mask. I'm not ordering my fellow Toa to accept this, Nokama, I am asking my brothers and sister to understand."

Vakama executed a perfect dive, hitting the water clean. A few moments later, he broke the surface, gasping for air. From below, he could see the airships moving slowly away.

Good, he thought. *I knew I could trust Onewa. He will make sure the ships get well clear of Metru Nui and the Matoran make it to safety. With luck, I won't be far behind.*

He turned and began to swim toward the Great Barrier. It was beneath the waters near that imposing wall of rock that he knew he would find the Vahi.

If Makuta has not found it already, he added grimly. *And if he has, it is too late for us all.*

From their vantage point aboard the airship, Nokama, Matau, and Nuju watched their friend begin his journey. "Mata Nui, keep him safe," whispered the Toa of Water.

"He will, sister," replied Matau. "Mata Nui loves ever-brave fools; that is why he made so many of us."

Nuju glanced at the Toa of Air and made a complicated series of clicks and whistles, punctuated by sweeping hand gestures.

"What was that?" asked Matau, puzzled. "I didn't quite catch it."

"He's been talking like that ever since we left Metru Nui," said Nokama. "It's the language of flying Rahi, or something close to it. The Toa of Ice has evidently decided that if we want a conversation with him, we will have to work for it."

"But will it be worth working for?" asked the Toa of Air.

Nuju made an abrupt slashing motion in the air and followed it with two shrill whistles.

"I think I've just been insulted," said Matau. "I would dare him to speak-say that again, but I wouldn't understand it the second time either."

Nokama laughed. After a moment, Matau joined in, and even Nuju cracked a smile. After so much danger and tension, the Toa Metru had finally become a team. Now they needed only Vakama to return to make them complete.

Be careful, Toa of Fire, Nokama thought. *I may not have visions of the future like you do, but even I can sense something terrible is waiting down there. Do not let it find you.*

Vakama took a deep breath and plunged beneath the waves for a third time. He had already realized he must widen his search area; the undersea currents could easily have carried the Vahi far from where it was dropped.

A Takea shark took notice of the new underwater presence and turned to get a closer look. Vakama saw the predator at about the same time. A moment's thought sent a wave of heat through the water, enough to frighten the shark away without doing any real harm to it.

The Toa of Fire scanned the sea floor, searching for the distinctive yellow gold of the Mask of Time. The rocky bottom was littered with the carcasses of dead Rahi, fragments of Matoran boats, and assorted other jetsam that had collected over the years. At one point, he thought he saw something gleam from amid the debris, but it turned out to be an old Kanoka disk launcher.

His lungs were beginning to strain. He wondered if perhaps this was a futile search after all. The Vahi might have been swept away to any point in the ocean, carried off by a Rahi, or simply been buried beneath the mud and silt and invisible to the naked eye. Odds were good it was lost forever.

Probably better that way, thought Vakama. *No being — not even a Toa — should command such power. Time is a fundamental force of the universe and the Vahi tampers with it. Even Mata Nui himself would not dare to do that.*

Resolved to give up the search, Vakama turned to head for the surface. As he did so, his eye caught a disturbance in the water. He changed direction to make a closer examination.

What the Toa of Fire saw was staggering. In a small area, the natural order of things had apparently gone insane. Plant life was growing at a fantastic rate, then dying before his eyes. Rahi that swam too close would stop dead, every life process seemingly suspended, for long moments before finally moving on. The effect seemed to come in waves, rippling a short distance through the water before dissipating.

Being careful to avoid the affected area, Vakama swam closer. Now he could clearly see the source of the bizarre changes. The Kanohi Vahi was wedged beneath a rock, a minute crack running along its side. It had changed color from gold to a dull orange, the result of expo-sure to the sea. Time distortions were emanating from it like waves of heat from a pool of molten protodermis.

The ache in Vakama's lungs reminded him he needed to surface. He shot upward, while the maskmaker in him debated what he had seen.

This makes no sense, he told himself. *If the mask is damaged, it shouldn't work at all. Even the tini-est crack wrecks a mask. Instead, it's pouring out power like I have never seen before, and if it sustains any more damage . . .*

Vakama caught a quick breath of air on the surface and then plunged back down again. A plan was already forming in his mind. As things stood, there was no way he could retrieve the mask. He would have to risk trying to repair it underwater.

He came as close as he safely could and began to count. He would only have a few seconds between time waves to act. His control would have to be pinpoint, or else he risked making things infinitely worse.

Concentrating harder than ever before, he sent an impossibly thin beam of fire at the mask. It struck at the base of the small crack, welding the two sides together. It was the work of an instant for the entire job to be done, but Vakama felt like a year had passed.

And with this mask, it very well might have, he reminded himself as he wrenched the Vahi free.

Pumping his legs furiously, Vakama made for the surface. He had a long journey ahead of him to reach the island above. With the only known water route blocked off, he would have to travel overland through one of the tunnels. With luck, the Rahi who had infested them had moved on to the surface.

He was calculating the quickest and safest way to travel when he felt the disturbance in the water. He glanced down to see a waterspout forming below him. It was rocketing up toward him at amazing speed. Knowing he could never outdistance it in the water, Vakama seized the only option he had.

With only a fraction of a second's hesitation, he slammed the Vahi over his mask. If he could muster the willpower, he could slow down time around the waterspout and buy a few moments to escape. He turned in the water to face the oncoming surge. It had picked up speed. Vakama struggled to settle his thoughts and focus on the mask, but it was already too late. The waterspout smashed into him like a pile driver, catapulting him out of the water and toward the Great Barrier.

Desperately, Vakama twisted his body to

absorb the impact. He crashed into the solid rock wall and began to slide back down toward the water. Too stunned to use his elemental or mask powers, he could only reach out and grab on to a ledge. Vision blurred, strength rapidly waning, he tried in vain to pull himself up.

Then there was someone else there. It was a huge figure, power radiating off of it, but not someone Vakama recognized. His first thought was that Makuta had found him, but the aura of this being was different somehow. He fought to make his eyes focus, but the collision with the Great Barrier had been too devastating.

"Help me . . . ," he said.

The figure stood over him, seemingly unsure of what to do. Then it reached down and ripped the Vahi off of Vakama's mask. Once it had the powerful Mask of Time in its possession, it lost interest in the Toa of Fire and began to climb the Great Barrier.

"Wait!" Vakama shouted weakly. But the figure never even looked back.

The Toa of Fire had no more time to worry about this. The world was rapidly going black. His hand lost its grip on the ledge, and Vakama fell down into the unforgiving sea. He hit the water, plunged deep beneath the surface, and did not rise again.

Far from Metru Nui, in a place never before seen by Matoran eyes, a lone being sat and brooded. His true name had not been spoken by anyone in more than two millennia. It was doubtful anyone even remembered it, or, if they did, that they would presume to be so familiar as to use it. Those who dared to address him called him the Shadowed One.

In the corridors outside his chamber, servants scurried to and fro as quietly as possible, lest they make a noise and disturb his meditations. Even the Dark Hunters training below his tower did so in unnerving silence. The last member of that order to shatter the peace with a shout had been moved into a new career as a practice dummy.

All who had seen the Shadowed One on this day knew it was a particularly bad time to risk his wrath. The reason was no secret: A short time before, he had dispatched two Dark Hunters, Nidhiki and Krekka, to the city of Metru Nui at the request of Makuta. Neither had returned, nor had Makuta been heard from. He was confronted with the very real possibility that his two operatives were dead.

He would not shed any tears for either. Nidhiki was a traitorous ex-Toa who had attempted to betray Metru Nui to the Dark Hunters ages ago and then fled the city when his attempt failed. Krekka was an idiot, worthwhile only for his brawn and his infantile sense of loyalty. No, losing those particular individuals was not the problem — what infuriated him was that anyone would dare to harm a Dark Hunter at all.

In all the centuries since the order had been founded, certain rules had remained unchanged. Dark Hunters would take on any employment if the reward were sufficient, regardless of the risk to themselves or others. Hiring a Dark Hunter without good reason or refusing to pay after the task was completed would bring immediate punishment. Slaying a Dark Hunter would bring the full force of the order down upon the offender. And now someone had dared to erase not one, but two, from existence.

The Shadowed One lightly tapped a crystal that hung suspended by his throne. In response, the dark, twisted creature that served as his Recorder crawled into the chamber and took up a position beside his master. It was the Recorder's job to preserve the wisdom of the Shadowed One for the ages, as well as to keep an account of the Dark Hunters' successes.

"I have pondered," the Shadowed One began, "and I have decided. The deaths of two Dark Hunters cannot go unpunished. Those responsible must be struck down as an example to others who might contemplate such action."

"Have you discovered who these offenders might be?" asked the Recorder, furiously scratching his master's thoughts onto a tablet.

The Shadowed One nodded. "There is only one group of beings who would be so foolish as to do such a thing: Toa. I do not yet know if it was Lhikan or some other of his kind in Metru Nui who committed this act, but whoever they are, they *will* pay. Sentrakh and I will travel there ourselves to see to this."

The Recorder paused in his writing, surprised. "You will go? You will not merely send more Dark Hunters?"

"Those who did this have obviously lost their fear of the order," the Shadowed One replied. "Respect is born from fear . . . obedience as well. And so fear must be restored in the hearts of those who would stand against us."

"Yes, yes, of course," the Recorder said. If he wasn't fully convinced of the wisdom of the plan, he certainly wasn't going admit it. "After all, what Toa could successfully oppose you? Your power is second only to that of great Makuta himself."

The words had barely been spoken before

the Recorder realized the error he had made. Slowly, he started to back out of the room, even as the Shadowed One's eyes blazed with anger.

"Second to —?" the leader of the Dark Hunters hissed, springing from his throne to grab the Recorder by the neck. "Understand this, scribbler — I am second to *no one*! Least of all that scheming, arrogant, walking scrap of shadow. . . ."

The Recorder would have apologized profusely had he been able to breathe. To his great relief, the Shadowed One decided he was not worth killing, and simply threw him the length of the room. The jarring impact was almost welcome compared to what the alternative would have been.

"Get out of my sight," ordered the Shadowed One. "Tell Sentrakh we depart immediately."

The Recorder scurried out of the chamber. After he was gone, the Shadowed One returned to his throne and remembered Metru Nui. For far too long, that city had been a thorn in his side. Perhaps, when its Toa had been reduced to helplessness, it would be time to remove that thorn once and for all.

The Shadowed One walked down a winding stone staircase that led to the training chamber. No one was scheduled to be using it at this time, but from the sounds of combat emanating from below, it was obvious that someone was. He had no doubt it would be the Dark Hunter he was seeking.

The Shadowed One paused in the doorway. Lariska was there, moving with the grace and agility of a Rahi panther as she spun, leaped, and plunged her twin daggers into wooden targets. Without breaking stride, she went into a roll, then sprang up to throw her dagger between the eyes of a mounted Muaka head.

"I thought you preferred live practice targets," the Shadowed One remarked.

Lariska retrieved her dagger and went into another routine, never looking at her visitor. "I do. Finished all of them. They're stacked outside." She did a midair somersault and sliced off the head of a mannequin. "Better do something before they start to smell," she added as she hit the ground.

"You are back sooner than I expected," said the Shadowed One. "Unable to carry out the mission?"

Lariska laughed sharply. "You know better than that." She jumped from a standing start into the rafters, executed a series of complicated gymnastic tricks, and then did a perfect dismount to land in front of her leader. The Shadowed One could not help but be a little amazed at her fluid skill, considering that her left arm was completely mechanical.

"Reporting," she said, making no effort to hide her sarcasm.

"The Toa?"

"Dead."

"The Turaga?"

"Fled."

"The payment?"

"In the vault."

"*All* of it?" the Shadowed One asked pointedly.

Lariska glanced at her mechanical arm, then back at the ruler of the Dark Hunters. "*All* of it. I remember my lessons well, Shadowed One, especially the painful ones."

The Shadowed One smiled. "I find it hard to believe even you could eliminate an experienced Toa so quickly. Tell me the tale."

Lariska shrugged, already restless. She liked to be moving all the time. Standing around and talking was torture for her, which is precisely why the Shadowed One made her do it. "Usual routine. I scouted him for two weeks. He was a Toa of Gravity. His standard response to an attack was to dodge the first strike and then erase the gravity around an opponent and send them floating upward. I practiced fighting in zero gravity using *levitation* disks, so when he tried that, I was ready."

A dark smile crept onto her lips. "And he wasn't ready for my being ready."

"I am leaving the island for a short while," the

Shadowed One said abruptly. It was better not to let his Dark Hunters dwell on their successes — it made them prideful and thus dangerous. "You will oversee things here in my absence."

Lariska couldn't take the idleness anymore. She did a backflip and executed a rapid series of feints with her daggers. The Shadowed One noticed that the blades were stained green, a sign that she had applied poison to them before the session.

"Why me?" she asked.

"Because the other Dark Hunters are afraid of you," he replied. "And you are afraid of me."

Lariska suddenly hurled a dagger in his direction. "Am I?"

The Shadowed One erupted into a blur of motion. He grabbed a dagger off of a table, threw it, and knocked hers out of the air. "If you are wise," he said, "then yes, you are."

"Where are you going?"

"That does not concern you."

"When will you be back?"

"When I return. In the meantime, accept

only those commissions that promise high reward. Keep the Recorder informed of all arrangements. And Triglax returned with only two pieces of equipment when the contract specified three. Have his quarters and usual hiding places searched, then teach him the error of his ways."

"What curriculum?" Lariska asked, already looking forward to her confrontation with the obnoxious Triglax.

"I want him able to walk on his own," the Shadowed One answered. "But unable to breathe without pain for, oh, six weeks. That should be sufficient."

"Hands?"

"Intact," he said. "I believe enough hands have been removed this year."

He started to go, then stopped. "Tell me, Lariska. If I turned my back on you right now, would I find a dagger in it shortly after?"

She shook her head. "No."

"Then, before—"

"That was . . . play," she answered, smiling.

"I know you. You would never turn your back on anyone without guards in the shadows ready to cut them down if they made a move. So, no . . . the day I kill you, Shadowed One, you will see it coming. I want you to see it coming."

The Shadowed One turned and walked away, confident that in his absence he was leaving the Dark Hunters in just the right pair of ruthless hands.

Vakama opened his eyes. The first thing he noticed was that he was not underwater. In fact, he was lying on a comfortable sleep pallet, staring up at a strangely familiar stone ceiling.

The second thing he noticed was that, for a Toa who had just been slammed into the Great Barrier, he felt great. His muscles didn't ache and his lungs seemed fine despite his almost drowning. Still, something felt . . . wrong. Granted, Toa had great strength and resiliency, but he felt almost too good. Almost as if the waterspout and the impact with the rock wall had never happened.

He sat up, and suddenly everything made

sense, and at the same time nothing did at all. His Toa armor was gone. His legs, arms, and torso were all shorter.

Vakama went numb with shock. How could this have happened? When? It shouldn't have been possible but . . . *I'm a Matoran again!*

Now he knew where he was. This was his home in Ta-Metru, a home he knew had been leveled in the earthquake that followed Makuta's efforts to seize power in the city. He had lived here for countless years, working first as a tool-maker and later as a maskmaker. His forge was only a short walk away, just past Takua's dwelling. For a moment, he wondered how Takua was doing these days.

"No! No, no, no!" Vakama shouted. "Takua is gone. He's with the other Matoran, asleep in the spheres and heading for the island above. My home is gone. My metru is fire, smoke, and rubble. And I . . . I am a Toa!"

"What are you shouting about?"

Vakama glanced up to see Jaller poking

his mask into the doorway. He looked none the worse for wear for a Matoran who had been kidnapped by Vahki and forced into a coma. For just a second, Vakama forgot the impossibility of the entire situation and felt a surge of joy at seeing his friend again.

"Jaller? Is that you?"

"Of course it's me, akilini-head. Who else would it be? You better get up or you'll be late for work."

"Work?" Vakama repeated, as if he had never heard the word before.

"Yes, *work*," Jaller replied, exasperated. "You know, that thing you do all day? That thing Takua is apparently allergic to? Work. And if you're not there on time, the Vahki Nuurakh will give you a wake-up call you won't forget."

Vakama hopped off the bed. "You mean the foundries are operating? The forges? When? How?"

"When have they ever stopped?" asked Jaller. "Hey, are you all right? You look like someone stepped on your favorite lava eel. Were you on the wrong end of a Vahki stun staff or something?"

"I . . . no, I don't think so," Vakama said quietly. "But I'm not quite myself today. Maybe I shouldn't go to work."

Jaller shrugged. "If you want to chance that, go ahead. But if Turaga Dume was expecting me to hand over the Mask of Time today, I think I would make a point of being at my forge."

Vakama almost lost his balance. *Turaga Dume? The Mask of Time? But the Dume who wanted that mask was Makuta in disguise . . . and the mask is . . . is . . .*

He looked around the room. There was no sign of the Kanohi Vahi. Then he remembered the hulking brute who had taken it from him as he clung to the rocks. At least, he thought he remembered that. If there was any truth to the memory at all, Metru Nui was in deadly danger.

"The Toa!" he snapped at Jaller. "Where are they?"

"Where they always are," the Matoran responded, edging away from the door. "They are at the Coliseum with Turaga Dume and Turaga Lhikan. The Toa of Fire is discussing ways to defeat the Morbuzakh plant."

"But I'm —" Vakama began. Then he caught himself. The world had gone crazy, and Jaller obviously hadn't noticed. Insisting he was a Toa wouldn't do anything but convince his friend he was crazy. Still, that left one very important question he wished he didn't have to ask.

"Jaller . . . who is the Toa of Fire?"

"You are a few flames short of a fire, Vakama. Everyone knows the Toa of Fire!" Jaller answered. "It's Toa Nuhrii!"

At one time, so many stunning revelations one on top of the other would have overwhelmed Vakama. But that was before he became a Toa in more than just name. He had overcome his insecurities and his fears. He had confronted the darkest part of himself during the struggle with the Visorak and emerged stronger for it.

Or did I? Did any of that happen at all? Was I ever really a Toa, or did I just dream it all?

Too many things did not add up. He grabbed his maskmaking tool and a stone tablet and began to burn a list of them all into the rock:

1. The Morbuzakh is still alive, when I know we destroyed it using the Great Disks.
2. Lhikan is a Turaga. But he became a Turaga when he turned Nokama, Nuju, Onewa, Matau, Whenua, and me into Toa Metru. And he's dead, killed in battle with Makuta.
3. The city is undamaged. There has been no earthquake. The Vahki are still functioning. The Matoran are still working.
4. Turaga Dume is running the city. But is it the real Dume, or Makuta in diguise?
5. Nuhrii is the Toa of Fire.

That last one was the hardest to take. During the battle with the Visorak, Vakama and some of the other Toa had discovered evidence that Nuhrii, Ehrye, Ahkmou, Vhisola, Orkahm, and Tehutti had been destined to become Toa Metru. Makuta had subtly influenced Lhikan to choose Vakama and his team instead. By doing so, he had gone against destiny and the will of Mata Nui, which perhaps explained the number of disasters that had followed. More than once, Vakama had wondered if some of the terrible events might have been avoided if Lhikan had made the right choices.

Evidently, he did, Vakama thought. *Somehow, everything that happened from before the time Lhikan helped us become Toa Metru has been wiped out. What could have the power to do that? The Vahi? But the legends of the Mask of Time said nothing about this sort of thing being possible.*

There was, of course, another alternative, one Vakama preferred not to think about. It was possible nothing had been erased or rearranged. All of his experiences as a Toa Metru might have been nothing more than a dream or hallucination. Everything — Makuta's betrayal of the Matoran, their capture, the Visorak, the Toa Hordika — might have been nothing but a delusion brought on by overwork.

Vakama shook his head. "No. I won't accept that. It was real. I *know* it was real. And I know the Matoran who can help me prove it."

3

Matoran from other parts of the city rarely traveled to Ko-Metru. It wasn't so much that Ko-Matoran were unfriendly, although they often were. It had more to do with the overwhelming silence that blanketed the district, day and night. Takua had once said that he always started speaking in whispers as soon as he crossed into Ko-Metru, although he was never sure why.

The last time Vakama had been here, the metru was deserted of everything but Rahi. The Knowledge Towers still stood but were badly damaged by the earthquake that had rocked the city. At least, that was the last time Vakama *remembered* being here — and there was certainly no evidence now that any of it had ever happened. Ko-Matoran filled the streets, the Knowledge Towers stood tall and proud, and even the chutes were running on time. Under ordinary circumstances, seeing the metru intact again would have been a dream come true. Today, it felt more like a nightmare.

Vakama was so lost in thought that he almost walked right into a huge ice sculpture. He looked up to see it was the figure of a Toa wearing a Great Mask of Illusion. Carved at the base was the name Toa Ehrye.

Of course, thought Vakama. *He would have been Toa of Ice if Lhikan hadn't chosen Nuju. More proof that either the universe has gone insane, or I have. I vote for the universe.*

On a quiet side street, he found the Knowledge Tower in which Nuju had worked as a Matoran. The scholars inside the front doors firmly insisted that he could not ascend to the upper levels for any reason. It was only when he mentioned bringing a piece of equipment that would make Nuju's telescope ten times more powerful that they agreed to let him pass. They were so excited by the prospect of a better view of the stars that they never even asked to examine the part, a good thing since it did not exist.

Nuju, a Matoran once again as well, was hard at work scanning the skies for astronomical evidence of Mata Nui's will. He didn't even turn around at the sound of Vakama's entrance.

"Whatever it is, leave it," said Nuju. "If you can't leave it, then take it back out with you. If it's too heavy to carry back out, then how did you get it in here in the first place?"

"Nuju, I need to speak with you."

The Ko-Matoran peered over his shoulder at his visitor. The eyepiece of his mask extended and retracted as he took a closer look. "You're Vakama, aren't you? The one who built the telescopic lens into my mask?"

"That's right," Vakama replied. "I need your help. It's about the Mask of Time."

That was enough to get Nuju's attention. "You finished it? Where is it?"

"I . . . don't have it with me. I need to know if there are any legends about the powers it is supposed to have."

Nuju flung his arms up into the air. "Legends! There are legends about everything,

Vakama. Sometimes I think all Matoran do all day is make up legends. Be specific."

"Nuju, I — something is very wrong in this city," Vakama began.

"I know. We're under attack by savage foliage," Nuju said acidly. "Is that all?"

"No, I mean things are not the way they are supposed to be. You . . . you should be a Toa!"

Nuju stared at Vakama for a moment in stunned silence. Then he burst out laughing. The noise sounded doubly loud because Ko-Metru was always so quiet.

"Me, a Toa? Not for all the purified protodermis in Ga-Metru," Nuju said, turning his back on Vakama. "All right, you had your little joke. You can leave now."

Vakama took three quick steps, grabbed Nuju, and spun him around. "I'm not joking! None of this should be here! The Knowledge Towers have been shattered, the power plant destroyed, the Archives broken open, and their Rahi on the loose in the city. I've seen it, and so have you! Don't you remember?"

Nuju nodded slowly. "Sure, Vakama. Whatever you say. And you think the Mask of Time had something to do with this? Well, I could be of more help to you if I could examine the mask. Is it somewhere you can get it?"

"No, I —" Vakama paused in mid-sentence. For less than a split second, the chamber had changed. The walls suddenly had great cracks in them. Ice bats were nesting in the ceiling. Nuju was not there. In fact, Vakama was standing alone . . . and he was a Toa.

As quickly as it had changed, the room flashed back again, becoming the neat, orderly workplace of a Ko-Matoran seer. Nuju was waving a hand in front of Vakama's mask.

"Hello?" asked the Ko-Matoran. "Are you in there? I don't think the Mask of Time is the problem, friend. I think maybe your own mask is on too tight. But go and get me the mask you made and I will see what I can find out."

Vakama was about to explain that he didn't have the mask, someone had stolen it. But he thought better of it before the first word was spoken. Something was telling him that maybe it was better if no one else knew about that — at least, not until Vakama had a better idea of what was going on in Metru Nui.

As it turned out, he wouldn't have had the chance to say anything to Nuju anyway. The Knowledge Tower observatory window was shattered by a squad of Vahki Keerakh. They stormed into the chamber and advanced on Nuju, stun staffs at the ready.

"No!" cried the Ko-Matoran. "I was working! He interrupted me! Look, I was right in the middle of —"

The Vahki staffs flashed. The power of confusion they contained took effect instantly, as Nuju lost all sense of where he was or when.

And he's not the only one, thought Vakama grimly as he ran from the room.

Vakama took a chute to Ga-Metru. Just like every other spot in the city, it looked perfectly normal. Scholars and educators traveled back and forth from school to school, most of them so buried in their notes, they could have walked into a giant Muaka without noticing.

He spotted Nokama talking with a blue Toa. As he approached, he recognized the hero as Vhisola, an old friend of Nokama's and evidently now the Toa of Water. She was giving the Matoran a pretty stern lecture.

"You should know better!" said Toa Vhisola. "All research and experiments have to be approved by a Toa. That's the law. If I reported you to the Vahki —"

"I know, Toa Vhisola," Nokama answered quietly. "Thank you for not informing the Vahki Bordakh, Toa Vhisola. I won't do it again."

"See that you don't." Vhisola caught sight of Vakama approaching and snapped, "What do you want, Ta-Matoran?"

"Just, um, passing through," Vakama answered, looking up into the Great Komau, the Mask of Mind Control, that Vhisola wore. "I had a delivery to make at a school near here."

Vhisola nodded, though she did not look convinced. "All right. I don't have time to waste talking to Matoran. I'll see you later, Nokama. Remember what I said."

The Toa jumped into one of the protodermis canals and swam off. Vakama watched her go. When he turned back, Nokama was walking quickly away from him. He had to run to catch up with her.

"Where are you going?"

"Back to work, Vakama," she said, not looking at him. "That's where I belong. I have . . . classes to teach, and . . ." Her voice broke.

Vakama put a hand on her shoulder. "What is it, Nokama? What's the matter?"

"Oh, it's just . . . it's my own fault," she said. "I was experimenting with energized protodermis, trying to figure out how it does what it does. But I didn't ask permission of Toa Vhisola first. You know that any new study has to be cleared by the Toa or Turaga Dume."

"Um, right," Vakama answered. "Remind me, why was that law passed?"

She looked at Vakama as if he had grown another head. "Why, to keep us from becoming

40

Toa, of course. After Vhisola and the others became Toa Metru using the Toa stones, they convinced the Turaga that six Toa were enough for one city. Just in case there was some other way for a Matoran to become a Toa, they banned all research to make sure no one accidentally discovered it."

"That's crazy!" Vakama snapped. When he saw a Ga-Matoran staring at him, he lowered his voice. "Becoming a Toa is destiny at work. You can't pass a law banning destiny."

Nokama shrugged. "Tell that to the Toa. My friend Onewa stumbled on an unexplored cave in Po-Metru, and Toa Ahkmou caught him. Ahkmou turned him over to the Vahki, and Onewa hasn't been the same since. He goes from work to home and back again and jumps at every shadow."

"Turaga Dume — the *real* Turaga Dume — would never stand for this," said Vakama.

"What do you mean, the *real* Turaga Dume? There's only one, you know."

"It's a long story," Vakama answered.

"Listen, I need your help. I'm trying to research the Mask of Time — what it can and can't do, that sort of thing. I thought you might know where there are some carvings about it, something the Knowledge Towers don't have."

"There might be something in the Great Temple, but I couldn't take you there," Nokama said. "If Vhisola or the Vahki caught us —"

"Then they won't. Maybe Onewa is in no shape to help us, but I'm sure Whenua and Matau would."

Nokama stopped in her tracks. "Matau? That's not very funny."

"What?"

"Vakama . . . Matau died a month ago, when the chute he was in was attacked by a Morbuzakh vine. Everyone knows that."

The two Matoran said nothing to each other for the remainder of the trip to the Great Temple. Vakama was more convinced than ever that someone had misused the Mask of Time and made all this happen. But if Onewa had become a coward and Matau had been killed, he was no longer sure even the mask could set things right again.

And that's assuming I ever find it, he reminded himself. *If I'm right and someone took it from me when I was a Toa, I still have no clue who that someone might have been. It didn't look like Makuta, but then, who knows what Makuta really looks like?*

"So you made the Mask of Time?" Nokama asked. "I mean, that is why you want to research it, right?"

"Yes, I made it."

"I hope you have a good hiding place for it. Otherwise, the Toa will be sure to take it from you."

Vakama chuckled. "It's so well hidden, even *I'm* not sure where it is."

"I'm serious," Nokama said sharply. "Maybe you should tell me where you hid it, just in case. You might think it's a safe spot and it's not, and I could suggest a better place. After all, you were never good at hiding things, Vakama — disks, tools, Toa stones, chute passes — I won every game of lose-and-seek we ever played."

Vakama glanced at his companion and smiled. "Yes, you did, didn't you? Except for that game near the Great Furnace — if the Vahki had come by that time, we would have both lost."

Nokama laughed loudly. "Um, yes, you're right. That was some game! I do remember that."

"I was sure you would," Vakama replied. "I've lost a lot of games lately. I think it's time I started winning some."

The two continued on their journey toward the spiritual center of the city. Vakama got a sudden flash of the Great Temple as a burned-out ruin and the surrounding protodermis canals cracked and leaking. He almost turned to look at Nokama, but then stopped himself, because he was not at all sure what he would see.

Lose-and-seek, he thought. *Is that what I'm playing? I lost my Toa power, my friends, my past, my whole reality, but where do I seek it? How do I get it back? And most important of all — who am I playing against?*

Sentrakh steered the boat unerringly toward the gateway that led to the Metru Nui Sea. It had been a long journey, but neither he nor the Shadowed One had slept. Having lived among potential enemies far too long to take chances, the Shadowed One rarely closed his eyes except behind locked doors. Sentrakh had no need for sleep or much of anything else beyond his duty.

Virtually all of the sea gates that led from Metru Nui to other lands had been closed by order of Makuta some time ago. Only this one remained open, by virtue of someone, or something, having torn the metal wide open. The Shadowed One guessed this was the work of Krekka, as he and Nidhiki made their way to Metru Nui.

As the boat sailed through the portal, a dull gray object caught the eye of the Dark Hunter leader. He ordered Sentrakh to halt and stepped out onto the narrow rock ledge that bordered the gate. A closer look confirmed his suspicion: This was a Kanohi Mask of Power he had spotted, a Mask of Speed, to be precise.

"Do you know what this is?" he asked Sentrakh. "A Kanohi mask — one of the most valuable possessions of a Toa. It no doubt belonged to some brave hero who ventured here from Metru Nui, looking to close this gate, thinking he was doing what was best for his city. He succeeded, but only after a great battle, and finally succumbed to his injuries. Only his mask was left behind."

The Shadowed One turned to look at his guardian, who was still staring straight ahead. "Did he find a hero's grave in these waters, do you think?" The Dark Hunter idly kicked the mask into the sea, watching it disappear beneath the waves. "Or just a final resting place in the mud for a fool?"

*　　*　　*

Vakama and Nokama knelt beside a canal and eyed the Great Temple. Vahki Bordakh were patrolling the site, just as they always had in the past. Ordinarily, Matoran could come and go as they pleased without too much trouble, provided that they stayed in the public sections. But the Ta-Matoran doubted that was the case in this new, harsher Metru Nui.

"We'll never make it past them," Nokama whispered. "This is foolish."

"No, we'll get in," Vakama assured her.

"You sound so confident."

"Why wouldn't I? I'm with you," he said, smiling. "Besides, I know a way in."

Vakama's memories of being a Toa Hordika included one occasion when he had slipped into the Great Temple past the Toa guards. It wasn't a very proud moment. He had gone there to kidnap and intimidate, all in the service of the vile Roodaka. He had been trying hard to forget those events, but he still remembered the route inside.

He led Nokama to a spot at the far end of the bridge leading to the temple. A partially hidden hatchway in the ground led down into an old pipe. It had once been used to transport purified protodermis from the Great Temple to the city but had been replaced years before by newer conduits. The pipe ran underwater and up into the center of the temple.

"You expect *me* to go in *there?*" Nokama asked.

"Think of it as a challenge," said Vakama. "Something to brighten up your quiet, boring Matoran life."

The pipe was narrow and dark and stank of damp. Little things were crawling along with Vakama and Nokama, but it was impossible to see what they were, which was probably for the best. As the pipe dipped below the sea, the pressure increased until it felt like two great hands pressing against their heads.

Finally, they made it out the other side, emerging in one of the Great Temple's protodermis purification chambers. Vakama motioned for

Nokama to follow him quietly, since there were Ga-Matoran workers in the room who wouldn't appreciate the sight of intruders. Together, they slipped through the shadows and made their way out into the corridor.

"Now where?" asked Vakama.

"Everything that exists on the Mask of Time is just legends," Nokama replied, looking around. She was obviously uncomfortable about being here. "No one even knew for certain that it could be made. How did you —?"

"Never mind," Vakama said. This was no time to go into the origin of a mask that he wasn't even certain he had created. He had carved the Mask of Time when he was a Toa Metru, but in this new world, he had never been a Toa Metru. That meant the Mask of Time he suspected had caused all this shouldn't even exist anymore. The paradox made his head hurt.

Nokama led him into a small chamber piled high with stone tablets. "All of this is sup-posed to go to the Knowledge Towers once it's translated," she said. "Most of it was brought by traders from other cities before the sea gates were closed. We've barely begun to catalog it, but maybe there is something here."

Methodically, the two Matoran began going through the tablets. Since Vakama could not read any of the inscribed text, he simply looked at any images carved on the stone to see if they looked like the Mask of Time. If they didn't, he put the tablet aside and went on to the next one.

After a while, he said, "How bad are things in the city?"

"Bad. Very bad," Nokama replied. "The Morbuzakh has taken over almost all of Le-Metru. Toa Orkahm made a valiant effort to fight it off, but he waited too long before acting. He's still recovering from his injuries. Without the work being done in that metru, chutes are breaking down and airships are grounded. The city is coming to a halt."

"Do the Toa have a plan to stop the Morbuzakh plant?"

"Toa Vhisola said something about finding

the Great Disks," Nokama answered. "But they can't seem to locate them."

Another paradox, thought Vakama. *I used the Great Disks to make the Mask of Time. In this reality, they evidently don't exist.*

He picked up another tablet, glanced at it, and felt a chill of recognition. The figure carved into its face resembled the being who had taken the Mask of Time from him on the Great Barrier.

"Who is this? What is this?" he asked.

Nokama took the tablet and began to read the carvings. "It's a . . . I think the name is Voporak. 'Very powerful . . . ,' I can't read this part, 'serves the Dark Hunters in order to . . . ,' " Nokama's eyes widened. "Vakama, it was bred to seek out the Mask of Time!"

"What? Tell me everything!"

"It has the ability to sense fluctuations in time, the sort it was believed the mask would create," she said. "If the Mask of Time came into existence, the Voporak would seek it out wherever it happened to be and seize it for the Dark Hunters."

Nokama glanced up at Vakama. "Why is this so important? Tell me the truth — have you seen this thing in Metru Nui? Now do you see why I said the hiding place is so important — maybe too important to be entrusted to you?"

Vakama nodded. "Maybe you're right, Nokama. Come with me. I think it's time the truth was revealed."

High atop a Ga-Metru roof, Sentrakh watched Vakama emerge from the protodermis pipe. If the unliving guardian of the Dark Hunter fortress was surprised by the identity of Vakama's companion, he did not show it. After all, it was not his place to have an opinion, merely to carry out orders.

The Shadowed One stood and pondered the pair of travelers wandering through the metru. At first, the scene made no sense to him. Why was Vakama wandering through a metru not his own? Where were the Toa he expected to find? Surely a Toa of Fire by himself could not have slain two Dark Hunters. . . .

Then an idle thought wandered through the Shadowed One's complex, twisted mind. He seized upon it, examined it, and followed where it led. He began to see the outlines of a plot almost as devious as one of his own. This Vakama was at its center, whether the native of Ta-Metru knew it yet or not.

"We follow him," said the Shadowed One. "He will lead us to the answers we are here to find. Once we have those answers, Sentrakh, you will dispose of him . . . in a way that will haunt the nightmares of Toa everywhere for ages to come."

"Where are you taking me?" asked Nokama for the sixth time.

"Po-Metru," Vakama replied. He had found an Ussal cart and persuaded the driver to let him borrow it. Under ordinary circumstances, an

Ussal driver would never let his vehicle or his animal out of his sight. *But these are far from ordinary circumstances,* Vakama reminded himself.

"Is that where the Mask of Time is hidden?"

"Something is hidden there," he said. "If I'm right, something just as destructive as the mask . . . something I had hoped never to see again."

"Speak plainly!" Nokama snarled. "Tell me where we are going and why, fire-spitter, before I —"

"Why, Nokama, calm down," Vakama answered. "Here I always thought you had the most patience of us all. You don't want to prove me wrong, do you?"

They crossed the border into Po-Metru. Roads gave way to pathways through the canyons, and buildings were replaced by low warehouses and shacks. The sounds of carvers' tools striking rock rang out all over the district. In the distance, Vakama could see a small herd of Kikanalo beasts on the move.

"It's really quite a remarkable place,"

Vakama muttered. "It's a shame we did not appreciate what we had."

"What are you talking about?"

"All this," he continued. "The metru. The Rahi beasts. The suns, the sky . . . Metru Nui was a beautiful place. The universe was well ordered and benevolent, all under the watchful gaze of the Great Spirit Mata Nui. We thought it would always be that way, so we didn't appreciate it while it lasted. None of us, not even you."

"Things change," answered Nokama flatly. "We can't always know the reasons for it. We have to trust that those with more power know what is right for us all."

"You mean like Toa Vhisola? I wasn't aware that Toa power automatically brought wisdom with it."

Nokama laughed harshly. "I was talking about real power, Vakama. Not the raindrops and wisps of a breeze Toa produce. The power to shape the future . . . the power to rule . . . the power to change the lives of others for all time . . . that is what I mean."

"What if those others don't want their lives changed? What if they're happy as they are?"

Nokama shook her head. "It makes no difference what they want. They will live in whatever world their superiors create for them, because it's all they know how to do. If Mata Nui had not wanted them herded, he would not have made them so easily led."

Vakama reined the Ussal cart to a stop. "Well, my leading you is almost at an end. Our destination is that cave over there."

"The Mask of Time is not in there," Nokama said stiffly.

"How do you know?"

"I just do. I'm not going in there."

Vakama was about to comment that it was a good thing, then, that he was the one driving. But before he could speak, the cart rocked violently, throwing him to the rocky ground. He looked up to see a Morbuzakh vine whipping through the air, about to grab him in its powerful embrace.

The sight brought back bad memories. The Morbuzakh plant creature had been created by

Makuta as part of his plan to take over Metru Nui. It had taken six Toa Metru armed with Great Kanoka Disks to stop it. Reduced to a Matoran, Vakama would have no chance against it alone. That fact made it all the more disturbing that Nokama was still sitting in the cart as if nothing were wrong.

"Nokama! Do something!" he shouted, narrowly avoiding the vine's blow.

"This is a bad place," the Ga-Matoran replied. "We should leave."

Now, there's *a shocking bit of news,* Vakama thought as the Morbuzakh went after him again. He picked up a rock and threw it at the vine. The Morbuzakh caught it in midair and smashed it on the ground. Dust and bits of rock flew into the air, blinding Vakama.

The plant creature saw its chance. Two vines snaked around Vakama and began to pull him toward the hole in the ground from which they had emerged. Vakama dug his feet into the ground and struggled with all his might, but could not break the plant's grip. In a matter of seconds, he would be below the surface and probably lost forever.

This was enough to rouse Nokama to action. She leaped off the cart with speed and agility Vakama had never seen before, charged the vine, and threw her arms around it. For a moment, he wondered if she seriously believed she could wrestle the Morbuzakh into submission. Then, to his amazement, the vines abruptly dropped him and retreated down the hole, trailing a thin stream of black sap.

Nokama turned to look at Vakama, but did not offer a hand up. "Now can we go?" she asked.

"You can if you like," Vakama answered, brushing himself off. "I have to see someone about a mask."

He climbed into the Ussal cart and took the reins. Reluctantly, Nokama took her place again beside him.

In a cavern far below their feet, the plant creature nursed its wound. The blue one had hurt it, although not badly. Still, pain had not been part of the arrangement. *It might,* the creature thought, *be time to reconsider this deal. I play a small role in this grand plot, it's true,* the plant-being continued. *And yet I may be the only one who knows the true power behind events. So I will wait, and I will watch . . . and Vakama will hear from me again.*

Vakama walked through the dark cavern, Nokama a step or two behind him. He had never been here before, only heard about the place from Onewa. Despite his assurances to his companion, he really had no idea if he would find what it was he was seeking here. But if this place was not the end of the journey, perhaps it would at least point him in the right direction.

He reached a dead end at the back of the cave. When Onewa had been here, an earthquake had weakened the stone, revealing a chamber beyond. In this strange, different Metru Nui, there had been no quake. Yet there had to be a way inside, and Vakama was determined to find it. He closed his eyes and ran his hands across the stone, searching for the part of the wall that did not feel quite right.

After what felt like hours, he found it.

There was a tiny, recessed portion of the rock that even someone as unschooled in caves as Vakama could tell was not natural. Taking a deep breath and steeling himself for whatever might come, he pressed on the stone.

The wall slid aside. Vakama saw something moving impossibly fast. Then it slammed into his face, adhering to his mask. He fell over, but never felt the impact. His mind was somewhere else, lost in a whirling haze of color and sound. Thoughts that were not his own invaded his mind. Memories of things he had never experienced washed over him. He fought to maintain his sanity against this mental assault. Finally, the pressure subsided and a form took shape in his mind's eye.

It was a Toa, that much was certain, but not one Vakama had ever seen before. His armor looked sleeker and more streamlined than that of a Toa Metru, almost like the carvings of ancient heroes Vakama had seen in the Archives. Yet somehow he sensed this Toa was not some figure from the past.

"I am Toa Krakua," the figure stated. "I greet you, brother, in the name of all the Toa who have gone before and all of those who have yet to be."

"What . . . what's going on here?" Vakama asked. "I've never heard of any Toa Krakua. Am I dreaming?"

The strange Toa shook his head. "No, Vakama, you are seeing as only you can see. Remember? You were gifted, even as a Matoran, with the power to see fragments of the future. I am one of those fragments, a Toa who will never come to be unless you succeed in your task."

"What task? What am I supposed to do?"

The Toa raised his sword. The tool began to vibrate and hum, and then sonic waves shattered a solid stone wall. "Find the truth, no matter what barrier blocks your way. Deception can strike you down, as surely as any blow from an enemy. You are a Toa without armor in a chamber of swords, Vakama, and only the truth can protect you."

Krakua paused, and then said, "You do not believe me."

Vakama was startled. He had doubts, certainly, about what he was seeing, but he felt that nothing in his expression would have betrayed them.

"And nothing did," said Toa Krakua. "I wear Kanohi Suletu, the Mask of Telepathy. Your thoughts are open to me."

"What truth am I supposed to find?" Vakama asked. "Why won't you speak plainly?"

Toa Krakua smiled. "The future can only share so much with the past, Vakama. That is a law even a Toa does not have the power to change."

"Isn't there anything you can tell me?"

"Two things will I share with you — I said before that if you fail, I will never exist. You must be prepared to fail, brother. If necessary, you must be willing to destroy the future and all that is now to stop evil from spreading."

"And the second?"

"Six heroes will one day be called upon to make a perilous journey into the darkest place you can imagine. They will brave the lightning . . . they will walk through the fire . . . they will stare into the eyes of evil, and if they waver even once, they will die. And you, Vakama, will bear the most terrible burden of all."

Vakama could see where this was going. "I will have to lead them."

Toa Krakua shook his head. "No, nothing as easy as that. You will have to send them on this quest, knowing they may never return . . . and knowing you can do nothing for them but wait and hope."

The mysterious figure opened his mouth as if to say more. Then a wave of shadow passed over him and he was gone, carried away by the darkness. Vakama's eyes snapped open and he realized with a start that he was still in the cavern. The creature was gone from his mask, but not very far.

"I thought you might prefer your Kanohi mask without this accessory." Turaga Lhikan stood there, holding the squirming thing in his hand. It looked like a cross between the small krana that lived inside Bohrok and the serpent-like kraata that lurked inside the creatures called Rahkshi. Vakama had seen such a thing once before, when it attacked Onewa near one of Makuta's lairs.

If it is here, then I've found the place I sought, he said to himself. *Now I just have to get out of here alive.*

"Are you all right?" asked Lhikan as Vakama rose to his feet.

"Are you dead?" Vakama replied.

"Of course not!"

"Then I'm not all right." Vakama looked around. The walls were covered in carvings. He tried to read them but they were in an unfamiliar language. He had a feeling even Nokama would have a hard time translating all this, and he knew better than to ask the Matoran who stood silently beside him. Long tables lined both of the walls, littered with Kanoka disks, fragments of ancient tablets, and other artifacts.

"It was lucky for you I was here," Turaga Lhikan said. "If I had not gotten that creature off of you —"

"I might have learned more than you want me to know," Vakama finished for him. "Your mask is excellent — I'm a maskmaker, I should know. But as always with items made by amateurs, you left a flaw."

Vakama sprang to one of the tables, grabbed a Kanoka disk, and flung it with all his might right at Nokama's head. Startled, the Matoran never moved. The whirling disk hit her mask — and passed right through.

Now Vakama knew what he had suspected was true: This wasn't Nokama. The instant he completely stopped believing that she was genuine, her form began to ripple and change. In fact, everything around him was changing and transforming, as the elaborate illusion he had been living abruptly collapsed. His own perspective on the world changed, too, and he now saw himself for what he truly was and always had been: the Toa Metru of Fire.

The image of Nokama was gone now, replaced by the reality of a Visorak Boggarak. It had been cloaked in an illusion of Nokama all this time, and her voice had been created by the power behind the ruse. Vakama felt a shadow fall on him and knew that behind his back "Turaga Lhikan" was changing, too.

No surprise, he reminded himself. *And whatever I must face, I will face it as a Toa.*

Slowly, Toa Vakama turned to confront his enemy.

Outside the cave, the Shadowed One and Sentrakh waited. It had been a long time since Vakama and his Boggarak companion had gone inside. To anyone else watching, it would have been a bizarre scene to see a Toa and a Visorak walking side by side, with the Toa having a one-sided conversation all the while. But the Shadowed One had seen this sort of thing before and was not easily impressed.

"I would have expected something more original," he said to Sentrakh. "It is an old strategy — if an attack on the body might fail, then attack the mind. I do not know exactly what Vakama was seeing or who he thought he traveled with, but it was all a sham, staged for his benefit. Now what could a Toa possess that would make someone go to such trouble to trick him?"

Sentrakh whirled at the sound of a heavy footstep on the rocky ground. In the distance, he could see the monstrous form of the Voporak coming toward them. The creature held something in its hand that gleamed even in the dim sunlight of Metru Nui.

It had taken the Voporak a long time to sense its master's presence in the city. The fulfillment of its life's purpose — the acquisition of the Mask of Time — had blinded it to any other concern. Now it came to present proof of its triumph to the one being it revered.

The Shadowed One saw his creature approaching and smiled. Even from far away, he could recognize the legendary shape of the Mask of Time. So it had come into being, at last . . . and the Voporak had done what it was created to do, track down and seize the mask from its owner.

Now it all made sense. Vakama's presence here . . . the complicated effort to convince him the world was not as he knew it to be . . . all one big trap to wrest knowledge about the Mask of Time from the unsuspecting Toa. And all the while, the mask itself was in the hands of the Voporak and about to become the property of the Dark Hunters.

The Shadowed One turned to Sentrakh and gestured toward the cave. "We have what they are seeking," he said. "We do not need them anymore."

Sentrakh nodded. A moment later, he unleashed a Rhotuka spinner at the mountain. It struck a boulder high above the cave. The result was a massive rock slide that buried the mouth of the cave.

"One less Toa to prove an annoyance," the Shadowed One said approvingly. "And as for the other . . . when we return, we will send a venom flyer to the Brotherhood of Makuta expressing our sympathy for their loss. They will brood and rage, but they will never be able to see our hand in this. And without proof, the Brotherhood will not risk a war."

The Shadowed One took the Mask of Time from the Voporak and admired its craftsmanship. It was hard to believe that this simple mask had enough power to change a universe — or destroy it. It felt good in his hand, as if it belonged in the possession of someone who would know how to use it.

And I do know, oh yes, the Shadowed One thought. *Soon, every living being will tremble at the news — the day of the Dark Hunters has arrived.*

The shock of the rock slide shook the cave, knocking Vakama off balance. He scrambled to his feet to find himself confronted by his worst nightmare.

The being who stood before him was an armored colossus who radiated power and evil. Crimson eyes gleamed with menace behind a rusted and pitted Kanohi mask. Great skeletal wings moved gently in a nonexistent breeze. His presence made every shadow in the cave seem deeper, every hope seem more distant, every bit of light seem suffocated by darkness.

"Makuta," Vakama whispered.

"Yes, little Toa," the giant rumbled. "Makuta, free to pursue my destiny once more . . . once I have the Mask of Time. I thought I'd get it from you with guile rather than force, but somehow you penetrated my illusion." He leaned forward, his eyes boring into Vakama's. "Tell me how."

The Toa of Fire took an involuntary step backward. "You were . . . sloppy," he said. "It almost worked. But then Nokama said something about how bad I was at hiding Toa stones — something that she and I didn't do until *after* we had become Toa. If we had never been Toa, how would she have known about it? That was what started me thinking. So I 'reminded' her of a game played near the Great Furnace — an event that never happened — and she recalled it well."

Vakama's hand edged toward a Kanoka

disk as he kept talking. "If she wasn't real, then was any of the rest of it? I had been thinking the Mask of Time caused all the changes, but if it hadn't . . . then something, or some*one*, else had. Since that would be a sadistic, cruel, demented thing to do, I naturally thought of you."

Makuta smiled. "Brave words from a Toa with no place to run," he said, gesturing toward the buried cave mouth. "But once I have the mask, I can easily free myself. Where is it, Vakama?"

"I don't have it," Vakama replied, bracing himself for whatever might come next. "It was stolen from me by a creature called Voporak."

In the past, Vakama had seen Makuta in triumph, in pain, angry, desperate, and defiant. He had never seen anything like the rage that now distorted the entity's features. Makuta was too furious even to form words. Before the Toa could move to defend himself, Makuta raised an armored hand and unleashed a shattering surge of dark energy, blasting Vakama into oblivion.

A jolt of pain awakened the Toa of Fire. Makuta had him by the arm and was dragging him through a stone tunnel like he was a load of broken tools headed for the reclamation furnace. Anger flared in Vakama. He'd had quite enough of being led around by Makuta. He willed the external temperature of his arm to shoot up several thousand degrees. Unprepared, Makuta released him with a cry of pain.

Vakama sprang to his feet, ready to fight. To his surprise, Makuta was laughing.

"You have spirit, little Toa," the armored figure said. "Spirit we will need in the coming battle." When Vakama did not respond, he added, "The Dark Hunters have something that belongs to me. I am going to get it back. And you are going to help me."

Now it was Vakama's turn to smile. "When

Makiki toads fly," he replied. "Why should I help you? What difference does it make to me if the Dark Hunters have it or you do? You're both foul."

Makuta grabbed Vakama by the throat and slammed the Toa against the wall. "Don't assume that all Dark Hunters are bitter ex-Toa like Nidhiki or bumbling masses of muscle like Krekka," he hissed. "Some of them would be enough to make my flesh crawl . . . if I had flesh."

Vakama lifted his arm and summoned a bright burst of fire. The sudden light blinded Makuta, forcing him to let go. As Makuta staggered back, Vakama followed up with more and more flares.

"You've been in the darkness too long," the Toa snapped. "Try a little light for a change!"

Makuta lashed out, striking Vakama and knocking him to the ground. "Enough!" bellowed the master of shadows. "While we squabble like Gukko birds, the mask we both covet may be on its way out of the city."

Vakama shook his head to clear it. He was

lying at Makuta's feet and at his foe's mercy, but the giant made no hostile move. "What are you saying?"

Makuta's eyes glowed bright red. "A truce, Vakama. Neither one of us attacks the other until the Mask of Time has been recovered. Once it is in my hands, if you are bound and determined to die fighting for it . . . I will oblige you."

Vakama didn't trust Makuta for a second. But he also knew that one Toa alone would not be able to defeat a team of Dark Hunters, and if Voporak succeeded in getting the Mask of Time out of Metru Nui, he might never find it again.

Suppressing a shudder of revulsion, Vakama said, "All right. You have a deal."

The two unlikely allies had been traveling for some time. Although Makuta had the strength to dig his way through the rubble, he was determined not to take a predictable course of action. There was another way out of this lair, he insisted, one that would give them the advantage of surprise.

Vakama found himself wondering where

the Rahaga and Keetongu might be, and if they might appear to tip the balance of power. It was possible that they might have left the city to go help Visorak victims elsewhere. But he hoped that was not the case. Any aid would be welcome right now.

Thoughts of absent allies made Vakama wonder about the blue Visorak that had posed as Nokama. It was not trailing behind them. "What happened to the Boggarak?"

"It exited another way," Makuta answered. "It will show itself to lure the Dark Hunters away, and no doubt be killed for its efforts. The world will not miss one Visorak, more or less."

"Your attitude is revolting."

Makuta paused and turned to face Vakama. "The Visorak know their place. They exist to serve those they are not powerful enough to defeat. You could learn from their example."

The master of shadows resumed walking. Vakama called after him, "As I recall, we *did* defeat you."

"A momentary setback, caused by my

energies having been divided," Makuta replied. "Absorbing Nidhiki, Krekka, and Nivawk, and overcoming their collective wills was more . . . distracting . . . than I'd expected. To put it in terms your simple mind would understand — I disagreed with something I ate."

He raised a hand to call a halt to their march. Vakama watched as Makuta grabbed a metal ring on a huge stone slab and began to lift it. Slowly, inch by inch, the rock began to move as Makuta pitted his power against the massive weight.

The Toa of Fire shrugged, pointed, and unleashed a blast of flame that melted the slab into a molten puddle. "Try my way," he said. "It's faster."

Makuta threw the metal ring to the floor of the tunnel. "You do have your uses, I suppose."

"I must, or you wouldn't need my help," said Vakama.

Makuta's mouth twisted into an evil smile. "Oh, yes, little Toa. You are the best kind of ally — one who is completely expendable."

*   *   *

Voporak stood, silently watching the buried mouth of the cave. The Shadowed One and Sentrakh had taken the Mask of Time and departed, leaving orders that Voporak should wait and deal with anything that emerged from the rubble.

An idle breeze swept through the canyon and stirred the pile of dust that a short time before had been a Visorak Boggarak. It had chosen a direct attack, evidently ignorant of its foe's true power. The touch of Voporak's hand had caused the Boggarak to live out its entire lifespan in a matter of seconds before disintegrating.

Any other being would have been bored or restless doing sentry duty in such a lonely and desolate spot. But Voporak felt no stirrings of discontent or any urge to be someplace else.

It had, after all, nothing but time.

Makuta and Vakama watched Voporak from high atop the rocks. "It doesn't have the mask," the master of shadows growled. "You said it did."

"I said it took the mask from me," Vakama corrected. "And maybe I could have gotten it back if I hadn't been playing your mind games."

"You were instants from drowning. I saved you. You wouldn't be here arguing now, if not for me."

Vakama bristled. "My city wouldn't be in ruins, my friends wouldn't be trapped in spheres, and the Mask of Time wouldn't have been at the bottom of the ocean to start with, if not for you!"

"Details. Trivialities. Your mind is cluttered with such things. Focus on the present," said Makuta. "This prize is too valuable for Voporak to be here alone — I suspect his master, the Shadowed One, is in Metru Nui as well. He must have the mask. Once we are past Voporak, we will run the Shadowed One to ground and take it."

Makuta waited a moment, then gestured toward Voporak and growled, "What are you waiting for? Destroy him."

"Toa aren't killers," Vakama replied. "If we were, we would have started with you."

"Very noble. Perhaps that explains why there are so few Toa around these days. Do you think Voporak would be so foolishly merciful? Or the Dark Hunters?" Makuta's next words were deadly quiet. "Or me?"

Vakama chose not to answer, instead drawing on his elemental power to create a white-hot fireball. He spent a long moment deciding who he would rather throw it at, and then hurled it toward Voporak. It flew straight and true, aimed perfectly to serve as a distraction.

The Toa of Fire readied himself to spring as soon as Voporak's attention shifted to the fireball. But to his surprise, the flames sputtered and died as soon as they came close to the creature. Voporak never even glanced in the direction of Vakama's attack.

Frustrated, the Toa tried again. Fire bolts, rains of flame, even a fiery cage, all were extinguished as soon as they came close enough to affect Voporak. Vakama muttered something that would have gotten him tossed out of a Ga-Metru school, which seemed to amuse Makuta.

"Watch," said the armored giant. He picked up a boulder and threw it at the seemingly invulnerable being. Mere inches away from Voparak's body, the rock crumbled to dust.

"What kind of power?"

"Time," answered Makuta. "Any force directed at Voporak ages before reaching it. Anything it touches grows old in its grasp, unless Voporak wills it otherwise. No power is immune to the ravages of the years, little Toa."

"Then how can it be defeated?"

Makuta's eyes narrowed. "It is a pawn. It is best handled by other pawns." The master of shadows gestured toward a canyon to the west. "Behold, Vakama — the sons of Makuta!"

At first, Vakama saw only a cloud of dust as if some great and terrible herd of Rahi were heading toward them. Then he began to make out forms and faces, and a chill ran through him.

It was a mob of Rahkshi, the monstrous creatures who dwelled below the Archives. There were hundreds of them, in dozens of different colors, all of them charging headlong at Voporak.

Vakama couldn't bear to look, and at the same time could not bring himself to look away. The first line of Rahkshi reached their enemy and collapsed as their armor disintegrated and the wormlike kraata inside them withered and died. Another wave followed, only to meet the same fate, followed by another and another. Still, they kept coming, heedless of their brothers' fates, marching blindly to their doom.

"They are born of my darkness," Makuta said, with what sounded like pride in his voice. "Each one carries a part of me within their gleaming armor. They live, and they die, in my name."

"If you controlled this kind of army, then why resort to trickery to capture the Matoran?" Vakama asked, horror-stricken. "Why not just unleash these monsters on the city?"

"If I had, there would have been no city left to rule," Makuta replied. "Now we must go, while my legions keep Voporak busy by dying at its feet."

When Vakama hesitated, Makuta grabbed him roughly by the arm and pulled him away from the spectacle. The Toa angrily shrugged off the grip and fell into step behind his hated foe. All through the long march down the mountain, Vakama did his best to ignore the angry hisses of kraata as they died.

At one time, not so very long ago, the Great Temple had been the grandest, most beautiful building in Metru Nui. Now it was a burned-out ruin, thanks to the Visorak. As he and Makuta approached, Vakama could not take his eyes off of the wrecked structure, as if it were a symbol of all the evil that had befallen his city.

"Ah, my brother's temple," said Makuta. "Once so glorious, now dead like the creatures upon which it is built."

The strange comment shook Vakama out of his thoughts. "Dead . . . what are you talking about?"

"Many centuries ago, a group of Matoran decided to grasp for greater power," the Dark One explained. "They exposed themselves to energized protodermis and became reptilian crea-tures called protocairns. They emerged from the sea just up there and destroyed the shoreline of Ga-Metru, including the Great Temple. Turaga Dume, the fool, had no idea what to do. Fortunately for the city, they died on their own. Their bodies merged together to form a new land mass, including the spit of dirt upon which the current Great Temple sits."

"Sounds like one of your plans," Vakama snapped.

Makuta laughed. "Little Toa, you have not yet begun to see even the barest outlines of my plans. I have schemes within schemes that would boggle your feeble mind. You may counter one, but there are a thousand more of which you know nothing. Even my . . . setbacks . . . are planned for, and so I shall win in the end."

The strange pair crossed the bridge that led to the Great Temple. Vakama could not help but remember his encounter with "Toa Vhisola" in Makuta's illusion. Ever since he had learned that six other Matoran were destined to be Toa Metru, and that his team was the result of Makuta's tampering with destiny, he had felt like a fraud. No matter how many heroic acts he and the other Toa performed, they would always know Makuta was responsible for their power.

"Why?" Vakama asked.

"Why are you a Toa?" Makuta answered. "No, I did not read your mind, Vakama — it is too quick a read. Your worries are transparent. I looked into the stars and saw the names of six Matoran destined by Mata Nui to be Toa: Nuhrii, Ahkmou, Vhisola, Tehutti, Orkahm, and Ehrye. Not a particularly heroic group, but weak-willed enough that they could have been molded by a strong leader like Toa Lhikan."

Makuta raised a hand, and shadows blotted out the stars. "And so I chose the six most argumentative, strong-willed, stubborn Matoran I could think of, and I planted their names in Lhikan's mind. He ignored destiny and chose you and your friends to be Toa Metru. I believed you would fail — as you ultimately will — and even if you do not, I have had the satisfaction of frustrating the will of Mata Nui."

Their conversation had brought them to the gates of the Great Temple. Makuta gestured for Vakama to go inside. "The Shadowed One must come here to learn whatever can be learned about the mask. You will wait in ambush. I have other matters to attend to."

Vakama considered arguing. He didn't trust Makuta out of his sight, especially not in a place still so filled with artifacts of power. But an argument would cost time, and time was something they did not have. He went into the temple.

Makuta waited until he could no longer hear Vakama's footfalls. Then he turned and said softly, "You can come out now."

The powerful Rahi called Keetongu emerged from the shadows of the temple. Makuta greeted his arrival with a grim smile of satisfaction.

Vakama had taken up a perch in the rafters of the temple, from which he could see the floor below. He rapidly grew restless. If the Dark Hunters did need information on the Mask of Time, he had no doubt they could go to other sources. *Perhaps Makuta just sent me in here to get me out of the way,* he thought.

He was about to climb down when he heard sounds of movement from below. He retreated deeper into the shadows and waited. A moment later, a bizarre figure moved swiftly through the chamber below. Vakama could not see it clearly, but the intruder was obviously a being of power.

Vakama sprang from rafter to rafter in pursuit, all the while thinking, *I really hate it when Makuta's right.*

Sentrakh heard the telltale sounds of a Toa trying to be silent. He did not bother to look up or give any indication that he knew he was being watched. He had a mission to fulfill in this ruined place. If a Toa, or a group of Toa, wished to watch him, that was no concern of his.

If they chose to try and stop him, they would be captured and brought to the Shadowed One. He would no doubt pry the secrets from their minds.

Regrettably, the heroes would have very little mind left when the process was done. That, too, mattered not at all to Sentrakh, beyond the pleasant anticipation of eliminating helpless Toa when the Shadowed One was finished with them.

Of such small moments of amusement was a happy life made.

Vakama had no idea who the creature below him might be, only that he had no business being in the Great Temple. He decided it was time to provide a "Keep Out" sign in words of fire.

The Toa concentrated. A jet of flame erupted from his outstretched hand, forming a fiery ring around Sentrakh. The yellow and black creature glanced at the fires, shrugged, and gestured toward his prison. Suddenly, the flames turned to stone. A kick from Sentrakh fragmented part of the rock ring, and he continued on his way.

One day, there will be an easy foe to fight, Vakama said to himself. *Just take its mask off and the battle's over . . . right, like that's going to happen.*

Vakama loaded his Kanoka disk launcher and took careful aim. Before he could fire, his target launched a Rhotuka spinner, and the rafter on which the Toa was perched disappeared. Vakama dropped like a stone and hit the floor of the Great Temple.

Sentrakh turned to see what he had caught. He was not impressed. The red Toa was staggering to his feet and taking uncertain aim with a disk launcher. Sentrakh decided it was easier to just keep his new foe distracted rather than engage in all-out battle. Another gesture surrounded Vakama in a sphere of darkness that even his flames would not dispel.

That was Sentrakh's first mistake. There was a time when impenetrable darkness would have been a barrier to Vakama. But during his time as a Toa Hordika, he had befriended the shadow and learned to use it for his own ends. Blinded to the world around him now, Vakama held his breath and listened.

Dripping water . . . the cries of Rahi birds . . . the groaning of the rafters . . . his mind sifted through all these and rejected them. There — the sound of metal scraping against stone. Vakama whirled and fired his Kanoka disk in the direction of the sound.

Sentrakh never saw the disk coming. One moment, he was functioning normally, the next he was 20 feet high and slamming his head into the rafters. A second later, a second disk hit and he was reduced in size to six inches. His concentration shattered, the darkness shrouding Vakama disappeared. The Toa took two quick strides and scooped up his enemy in his hand.

Now it was Vakama's turn to have assumed victory too soon. Even reduced in size, Sentrakh's power had not diminished. Calling on his molecular transmutation abilities, he turned the muscles shielded by Vakama's armor into solid protodermis. The effect spread slowly throughout the Toa's body, paralyzing him, and he knew there was worse to come. If Vakama could not find a way to stop the change, his organs would turn to stone as well. Soon, he would be a new piece of very dead statuary to decorate the Great Temple.

*   *   *

Makuta eyed Keetongu. The Rahi's shield array was rotating rapidly and his bladed tool was raised in preparation for combat. He could obviously sense the evil in Makuta and it was driving him into a rage.

"So. You are the one who destroyed Sidorak," the master of shadows whispered. "Now you follow me here from Po-Metru, no doubt intending the same fate for me. Unfortunately . . ."

Coils of solid shadow leaped from Makuta's hand and wrapped themselves around Keetongu, constricting him.

"I am not Sidorak," Makuta finished.

Keetongu was an instinctive fighter, not a strategist. Now his instincts told him that these bonds were tied to the will of his attacker. No amount of struggling would shatter them — it was the mental focus of his enemy that had to be targeted. Snarling, Keetongu charged and slammed into Makuta's armored form, knocking his foe off his feet. Robbed of the concentration needed to maintain them, the bonds vanished.

"You dare?" spat Makuta, rising. He hurled another bolt of darkness, but this time Keetongu was ready. The Rahi absorbed the energy with his shield, channeled it through his armor, and shot it back at Makuta in a Rhotuka spinner.

The spinner struck home. Keetongu advanced to follow up his score, only to find his enemy unhurt.

"You cannot harm me with my own power, beast!" Makuta said. He grabbed Keetongu's wrist and began to force the rapidly spinning shields toward the Rahi's throat. "Let us see if the same can be said for you."

Voporak surveyed the canyon. Its rocky floor was littered now with thousands of fragments of Rahkshi armor and the withered husks of countless kraata. Makuta's creatures had kept coming for hours, until finally their numbers were depleted.

He felt no sadness at the sight, only irritation. These things had no chance against him, after all, and it was a waste of time making him prove it.

Or was it?

Voporak glanced at the cave mouth. It was still buried in rubble. With suspicion nagging at the back of his mind, he bounded up the rocky slope. The first thing he saw was the melted slab of rock through which Makuta and Vakama had escaped.

So it had all been a trick, he realized. Rather

than face him in battle, Makuta and the Toa had dishonored themselves by fleeing, and dishonored him in the eyes of the Shadowed One. For that, they would get the rare privilege of watching as their lives sped by in seconds and death rushed to claim them.

Voporak looked down at the rocks. Tiny scratches and scrapes in the stone revealed where his enemies had walked. He would track them until they fell. Then he would make sure they did not rise again.

All Ta-Matoran maskmakers were, at heart, mathematicians. Getting a mask exactly right was a matter of figuring the precise volume of liquid protodermis needed, the proper angles of the carving, and a hundred other calculations. It was that solid background in math that enabled Vakama to know with certainty that he had only 9.6 seconds to live.

The Kanoka disk power had worn off. Sentrakh was back to full size and had not wavered since beginning his attack. Vakama guessed that total focus was required to maintain the flow of energy that was turning him to stone. What was needed was something to break Sentrakh's concentration — or just break Sentrakh.

The transmutation effect had not yet reached Vakama's eyes. He cast them about looking desperately for an answer. Almost ready to give up hope, he spotted something two chambers away, or thought he did. From where he was, it looked like a black vial, the same kind that the Toa Metru had once used to collect energized protodermis. Ga-Matoran had experimented with that substance in the past, trying to artificially recreate it. If there was energized protodermis in that tube . . . and if it was flammable . . . and if he could do something about it before his time was up . . .

There was no time to worry about the odds. As it was, Vakama needed to buy an extra two seconds for his plan to have a chance to work. Fortunately, Sentrakh's power was affecting only Vakama's body, not his mind. He mentally triggered his Kanohi Huna and turned invisible. As he did so, he fought the stiffness in his wrist and moved his hand ever so slightly, sending a thin beam of fire from his index finger at the vial.

Startled by the disappearance of his target, Sentrakh let up just slightly on his attack. His first thought was that the Toa had been teleported somehow. He never noticed the narrow jet of flame until it was too late.

Fire struck the vial, superheating its surface. The temperature of its contents rose by several thousand degrees. Pressure built up in the sealed vial with no way to escape, as precious seconds ticked away.

If this doesn't work, I'm my own stone memorial, Vakama thought. *But if I get really lucky, I only have to worry about being blown through a wall by an explosion. It's certainly good to be a Toa again!*

Makuta threw all his strength against Keetongu. The Rahi fought back with his own enormous might, with the rapidly whirling shield array between them. It was a deadlock, and with these two entities involved, it might last for eternity.

Then the master of shadows did the unexpected. As Keetongu bore down upon him, Makuta suddenly stopped fighting. With no more resistance, the Rahi could not keep from being propelled forward by his own strength. Makuta rolled backward, hurling Keetongu over him and slamming the Rahi onto the ground.

Before Keetongu could react, Makuta struck again. Heat vision shot from his eyes and struck Keetongu's armored chest, welding shut the compartment that hid his Rhotuka launcher. Robbed of his ability to use that tool, Keetongu had no way to release any energy he absorbed.

"I see fear in your eyes, beast," said Makuta. "Perhaps now you see that Sidorak's power was a mere fraction of my glorious darkness. How do you think the Rahaga will feel when they discover the body of their mighty Rahi ally? Will they mourn you, or just decide it is one less animal to clean up after?"

Keetongu lashed out with his pickax and landed a solid blow. Makuta grunted and unleashed chain lightning against the tool, sending electricity coursing through Keetongu's frame. Makuta's metallic wings carried him up off the ground and he hovered above his fallen foe.

"Now, how best to finish you off? Carry you out to sea and dash you against the rocks? Stake you out and leave you for hungry Rahi? So many things to choose from, but then the future ruler of the universe must get used to making difficult decisions. I believe I will select —"

An explosion ripped through the Great Temple. The shockwave struck Makuta in midair, sending him tumbling end over end out to sea. Keetongu, too, was blown away, barely catching on to a rocky cliffside with his pick. Neither was in any condition to see Vakama and Sentrakh come flying out of the building.

The Toa of Fire lay on the ground, waiting for the pinwheels of light to stop flashing in front of his eyes and the gongs to stop going off inside his mind. His Toa armor had come through the explosion largely unscathed, but the muscle beneath it was aching. Sentrakh lay nearby, unmoving. Vakama doubted his enemy was dead — he wasn't sure the thing even *could* die — but it seemed no threat now.

He painfully rose to his feet. In the distance, he could see Makuta winging his way back to the Great Temple. He was stunned to spot Keetongu climbing over the edge of the cliff, looking like he had been stepped on by Tahtorak. Before Vakama could call out to him, the great Rahi collapsed, unconscious.

Vakama started running toward his fallen ally. He had gone only a few steps when a block of solid, crystalline protodermis formed around his feet and ankles and he toppled forward onto the hard ground.

"No need to hurry, Toa," a voice said behind him. "Your race is over."

At first, Vakama thought this was the betrayal by Makuta he had been expecting. But Makuta was still far out to sea, though closing fast on the Great Temple. The Toa rolled over onto his back and saw two figures looming over him. One was Voporak, the other a monstrous being carrying a spear and one thing more: the Mask of Time!

"I am the Shadowed One," the being said in a harsh whisper. "Doubtless you have not heard of me, but you knew two of my agents: Nidhiki and Krekka. You and your kind killed two Dark Hunters, Toa, and now you must pay in kind."

Twin beams shot from the Shadowed One's eyes. Halfway to Vakama, they mysteriously disappeared in midair, only to reappear several yards away. They struck part of the Great Temple and that section vanished from existence.

A winged shadow fell over Vakama. Makuta had arrived.

"Why do you interfere, great Makuta?" the Shadowed One demanded, saying "great" as if the term was an insult.

Makuta alighted on the ground. "Because it amuses me to do so. A simple trick, to teleport your eyebeams from the air and redirect them as I chose."

"Beware," said the Shadowed One. "The

Dark Hunters have a right to revenge. You will not save this Toa."

Makuta's eyes glittered with malice. "The Toa? What care I for a Toa? If you want his life, you may have it — give me the Mask of Time and he is yours."

Wonderful, thought Vakama. *Two of the most evil beings in existence and I'm stuck between them. Here's hoping they don't decide to split the difference, and me along with it.*

The Shadowed One shook his head. "Ah, so you value this little bauble, do you? I would be unworthy of my high office if I deprived the Dark Hunters of such a powerful tool. I am afraid, great Makuta, that I must keep the mask, and the Toa."

"Unacceptable," Makuta replied. There was no implied threat in his voice. There was no need. He was Makuta — his very existence was a threat to all who lived.

The Shadowed One gestured toward Voporak. "We are two to your one."

Makuta unleashed blasts of shadow energy,

not at his foes, but at the ground beneath their feet. A great pit yawned before them and only swift reflexes kept Voporak and the Shadowed One from falling into what might have been their grave.

"A hollow advantage, Dark Hunter, when that 'one' is Makuta," said the master of shadows. "I *will* have my mask."

Vakama felt like he had walked into a realm of madness. Makuta was power personified, and this Shadowed One was provoking him. Voporak's abilities tampered with a fundamental force of the universe, and Makuta did not seem to care. A full-scale conflict would destroy Metru Nui, unless he did something about it. He willed the imprisoned parts of his body to superheat, hoping to melt or shatter his bonds, all the while watching the conflict brew around him.

"The Mask of Time, and this Toa's life, are my compensation for the loss of two Dark Hunters," said the Shadowed One. "They were sent here at your request and did not return. That cannot go unpunished."

Vakama felt himself rising into the air. Makuta had negated gravity underneath him and he now hovered between the two villains.

"If it must be, it must be," Makuta sighed. "Very well. Kill the Toa, if it will satisfy your need for revenge, and then we two will discuss the fate of the mask like civilized beings."

Vakama had heard enough. He was a Toa, not some trinket to be bartered over at a market. Anger fueled his fire, and the solid protodermis that bound him shattered, sending fragments of crystal flying everywhere. Startled, Makuta lost control of gravity and Vakama fell, twisting in midair to land on his feet.

The Toa of Fire took a step back, raising both hands, palms out, and pointing them at Makuta and the Shadowed One. White-hot flame swirled in his palms, just waiting to be launched at his foes.

"This stops now," he said. "My city has suffered enough at the hands of such as you."

"Foolish Toa," replied the Shadowed One.

"Any of the three of us could cut you down where you stand in an instant."

"That will be an instant longer than I need to turn you to ash, Dark Hunter," said the Toa. "So who wants to be first?"

The Toa looked from Makuta to the Shadowed One and back again. As he expected, both were waiting for the other to make the first move and pay the price for it.

"You say you want to avenge Nidhiki and Krekka," Vakama continued. "Then take a hard look at Makuta. Recognize anything?"

The Shadowed One looked at the winged, armored figure who stood before him. He had seen Makuta in different guises before, but now that he examined him closely, he could see parts of the master of shadows were disturbingly familiar. It seemed as if Makuta had become an amalgamation of himself, Nidhiki, Krekka, and some other creature, a situation that was only possible if —

"*You* killed them!" the Shadowed One

hissed. "You summoned Dark Hunters to your side and then sacrificed them to your own insane ambitions. Even a member of the Brotherhood of Makuta cannot treat the Dark Hunters this way! Now it is to be war between us!"

Makuta shrugged. "And to the victor goes the mask. Shall we?"

"We shall," the Shadowed One replied. At his signal, Voporak advanced. Makuta readied himself for that being's attack, taking his eyes off the Dark Hunter leader for a crucial second. The Shadowed One used that moment to strike, his eyebeams disintegrating Makuta's wings. The master of shadows bellowed in pain.

Forgotten in the conflict was Vakama, who took advantage of the respite to check on Keetongu. The Rahi was badly weakened but still alive. Vakama had no doubt that whoever won the fight would target him and Keetongu next, unless he gave them something better to do.

Voporak had moved in on Makuta. Even the master of shadows was at a disadvantage against a foe that could use time as a tool. Rather than strike out at him, Makuta was using his mind-reading power to anticipate and dodge Voporak's blows. All the while, Makuta strategized, looking for a weak point in his enemies' defenses.

"First *you* will fall, then the rest of your Brotherhood," vowed the Shadowed One. "With the Mask of Time in my hands, no one — not you, not the Toa — will be able to stop the Dark Hunters."

Then I will have to get it out of your hands, thought Vakama. He attached his Kanoka disk launcher to his back and triggered its flight pack function. But instead of heading toward the fight, he rocketed high into the air over the ocean.

Voporak landed a glancing blow. Pain wracked Makuta where his foe had touched him, as that small portion of his form aged rapidly. The shock took his breath away . . . and suddenly he had the answer.

When Voporak charged again, Makuta summoned his ability to create a vacuum. Accelerated time would affect almost any kind of power, but this was not an attack vulnerable to the passage of years. No amount of time would create air where there was none, and even Voporak needed to breathe.

The Shadowed One saw his minion stumble, trying in vain to fight off the lack of air. The leader of the Dark Hunters aimed his spear at Makuta and unleashed a blast of solid protodermis. The crystalline substance bound Makuta's arms to his sides.

"This held you before. It will do so again," said the Shadowed One. He held the Mask of Time high to taunt the master of shadows. "Perhaps I will even allow you to live, to witness my conquest of time itself."

This was the moment Vakama had been waiting for. He went into a screaming power dive, aiming straight for the Mask of Time in the Shadowed One's hand. Moving so fast that he was only a blur, he swooped down and snatched the mask from the Dark Hunter leader and rocketed off with it.

Enraged, the Shadowed One hurled his eyebeams at the fleeing figure. By chance, they struck Vakama's flight pack, badly damaging it. The Toa Metru spun out of control.

"Go after him!" the Shadowed One barked at Voporak. But the time-bending being was no longer listening. Makuta's vacuum had starved his brain of air and he had collapsed.

"Then I will do it myself," said the Shadowed One. He turned away from Makuta, saying over his shoulder, "And when I have that Toa's mask on the end of my spear, I will return to deal with you."

The Shadowed One took three steps before the sound of Makuta's voice stopped him.

"Dark Hunter."

He glanced behind to see his enemy still bound.

"If you believe you can 'deal with' me," the master of shadows said, "then you know nothing of Makuta!"

With that, the armored figured flexed his muscles and shattered his protodermis bonds. Then he advanced on the Shadowed One, his crimson eyes raging. The Shadowed One hurled more solid protodermis, only to have Makuta bat it aside. In desperation, he launched his eyebeams and dissolved a portion of Makuta's breastplate. But still the master of shadows kept coming, never hesitating for a moment, his eyes locked on the Shadowed One's.

"You have challenged me," Makuta said coldly. "Wounded me. Imprisoned me. Dared to place your petty ambitions above my wishes. You sought to make time your ally, Shadowed One — now let it be your death!"

Makuta lifted the Shadowed One high into the air and hurled him at the prone form of Voporak. As soon as he struck his minion, Voporak's defensive time field took effect. The Shadowed One could feel countless years slipping by him, his body weakening, his final moments now a yawning chasm before him.

Satisfied, the master of shadows turned and stalked away toward Ta-Metru. Vakama had been heading in that direction and he still had the Mask of Time. The moment had come to deal with that annoying Toa, once and for all.

Behind him, a now-ancient Shadowed One succeeded in pushing himself away from Voporak. He had aged perhaps three thousand years in a matter of seconds. He could not be sure how much time he had left in this life. But as he watched Makuta depart, he vowed that every moment of it would be devoted to making the master of shadows pay for this moment . . . and pay . . . and pay.

9

Toa Vakama was about to die.

His flight pack was so badly damaged that it would not even function as a Kanoka disk launcher anymore. He was spiraling out of control, headed for the pile of rubble that used to be the Ta-Metru Great Furnace. There wasn't so much as a puddle of water down below that he could aim for. His only consolation was that the Mask of Time would be smashed beyond repair by the fall.

He was just realizing why that would be a very bad thing — even worse than his dying — when the ground started to shift underneath him. All of a sudden, it did not look like pavement and stone below, but more like a nest of snakes that had been disturbed. No, that wasn't right either — those things writhing below him weren't greenish black serpents — they were vines!

This is impossible, Vakama thought. *Another of Makuta's tricks. The Morbuzakh plant is gone. We killed it in the Great Furnace!*

Then there was no more time for questions. He crashed to the ground, but without the shattering impact he expected. Instead, the vines had formed a bed of sorts underneath him. As he struggled to recover his senses, they wrapped around him and dragged him down below the street.

Vakama's eyes were taking too long to adjust to the darkness. He summoned a small jet of flame from his hand to light the surrounding area, only to have the vine around his wrist yank hard.

"No fire," a voice whispered. Vakama knew that voice, laden as it was with the feeling of death and decay. It was a voice he had never thought to hear again.

"Karzahni . . . ," he breathed.

The vines released him and slithered away. Now he could see the dark mass in the corner, looking like a monstrous, half-dead tree. The Karzahni had been Makuta's first attempt to create a plant creature, but the result had been a being too willful and stubborn to serve Makuta's ends. The master of shadows had exiled it from Metru Nui, where the Toa Metru first encountered it some time later. The Karzahni had blackmailed the Toa into retrieving a vial of energized protodermis for itself, and then died when that substance caused the plant to burn up from within. Later, the Toa used parts of the plant creature to keep their boat buoyant on the return trip to Metru Nui.

"You're dead," said Vakama. "This is another illusion. I have had enough of Makuta's madness."

"As have I," the Karzahni whispered. "But I am very much alive. I am of the earth and the green, Vakama — I do not die as flesh dies."

"I don't understand."

"When you submerged parts of my former self in the liquid protodermis of the sea, a tiny shoot grew from within. In time, that tiny piece of plant matter grew into a new Karzahni, with the memories and intelligence of the old. I am reborn."

The Karzahni obviously expected some momentous emotional reaction from Vakama. But the Toa had been through so much the last few days, all he could manage was a flat, "Good for you. What are you doing here?"

"Not everything you saw before was an illusion," the Karzahni replied. "Makuta and I achieved a truce and I agreed to play at being the Morbuzakh to make his false world more convincing. But now he is coming for you, Toa, and you have not the power to defeat him. You need an ally."

"Thanks anyway," Vakama replied acidly. "I've had one ally too many this trip. Unless you have some awesome Toa tool hidden in all that foliage, I don't see —"

"I have the ultimate weapon against Makuta," the Karzahni said, vines rustling and slithering about the chamber. "The truth."

One of the vines reached up and tore a chunk of rubble loose. Vakama looked up and saw the sky above Metru Nui ablaze with stars.

"You cannot fight him, Vakama, because you believe you were not meant to be a Toa," the Karzahni continued. "Makuta looked up at the stars and saw that Nuhrii, Ahkmou, and the rest were to be Toa Metru, and so he convinced Toa Lhikan to empower six other Matoran. He wanted you and your contentious friends to be the new Toa. That is what you have been told, is it not?"

Vakama nodded.

"And it is all the truth," the Karzahni said. "It happened just like that. Still, someone did lie, Toa, and that lie brought you into being."

"Who?" asked Vakama, intrigued in spite of himself. "Makuta? Lhikan?"

Another vine moved, winding its way slowly upward. Vakama watched it as it pointed up to the sky. "The stars," Karzahni said softly.

"The stars lied. They told Makuta that Ahkmou should be Toa of Stone, Vhisola Toa of Water, and so on, and he believed them. In an attempt to alter destiny, he planted your name and the names of your friends in Lhikan's mind so you would become Toa Metru. But have you never wondered, Vakama . . . *who planted your names in Makuta's mind?*"

Vakama's head was spinning. If what the Karzahni said was true, then Nuhrii, Ahkmou, and the others had never been meant to be Toa — the message in the stars had been false. It had all been a trick played on Makuta. But who would have the power to alter the path of the stars, except —

"Mata Nui?" Vakama said, stunned.

"The Great Spirit," Karzahni replied. "The Great Spirit who had been struck down by Makuta's treachery and knew that his only hope of recovery was to get the Matoran out of this city before it was too late. To do that, he needed Toa Metru, but he knew Makuta was watching the stars. The master of shadows would do anything to prevent those new Toa from coming into being."

It was all becoming clear to Vakama now. "So Mata Nui deceived him. He made the stars name six other Matoran to be Toa, insuring Makuta would never allow them to be given power. And then he planted in Makuta's mind the names of the six who truly were intended by destiny to be Toa."

The Karzahni chuckled, a sickening sound. "Believing himself to be thwarting Mata Nui's will, Makuta turned around and used his powers to influence Lhikan into making you and your friends Toa Metru — the very Matoran Mata Nui had wished to be heroes all along! The Great Spirit knew there was only one way to make sure the six destined for greatness would have the chance to be Toa Metru, and that was to trick Makuta into making it happen himself."

Vakama sat down on the stone floor, still trying to accept what he had just learned. All his life he had heard of the glory of Mata Nui and how he was responsible for the sun that shone and the breezes that blew and all the gifts nature had given the Matoran. But in all that time, he had never heard of the Great Spirit intervening directly to make things right. Now, more than ever, he realized what a crime it had been that Makuta had cast Mata Nui into unending sleep.

"Wait," said the Toa of Fire. "Wait a moment. I saw a Toa disk with Nuhrii's mask on it. Nokama saw Kanohi mask niches with the names of the other six Matoran. How is all that possible, if they were not meant to be Toa?"

"Ah, Vakama — your fire burns so bright, yet you remain so blind," Karzahni chided. "Makuta has his Brotherhood, the Shadowed One his Dark Hunters . . . has it never occurred to you that there are some in this vast universe who are sworn to the service of Mata Nui, and he alone? It was they who manufactured the evidence to help convince Makuta, and they did a masterful job, it seems."

It made sense, and it was certainly easier

to accept than the idea of Ahkmou as a Toa. But one question still remained unanswered. "How do you know all this, Karzahni?"

The plant-thing laughed as if at a private joke. "Oh, one of those servants of Mata Nui's will happened to wander too close to one of my tunnels some time ago. He told me the whole story, all that I have just told you, before he died."

A dozen more questions sprang to Vakama's mind. *What was this mysterious order whose members apparently knew the will of Mata Nui? How many were there, and how long had they been in Metru Nui? Lhikan had never spoken of them, nor had Turaga Dume — was it possible even they did not know this group existed?*

He wasn't going to get answers from the Karzahni. A bolt of shadow came from above and struck the plant-thing dead center. Darkness spread like a plague down its vines and branches, forming a chitinous shell that covered every inch of the plant. In a matter of moments it was completely trapped inside, cut off from all heat and light.

Vakama looked up. Makuta was above,

staring down through the hole in the chamber ceiling. The breastplate of his armor was damaged and greenish black energy was leeching out of him. A faint wisp of shadow drifted from his open palm, the remnants of the power used to fell Karzahni.

"Come out, little Toa," Makuta said. "If I have to come in after you, it will be most unpleasant."

Vakama hurled a fireball, but not at Makuta. Instead, he threw it against the far wall, melting a hole in the stone. He jumped through the gap and found himself in an Archives tunnel, one of several that stretched beneath Ta-Metru. He ran then, while behind him an angry Makuta smashed down what remained of the wall.

Bolts of chain lightning flashed around Vakama as he hurtled through the narrow passages. He could hear Makuta's heavy tread behind him, coming nearer all the time. At some point, the master of shadows was going to catch up to him, and then what? As Karzahni had said, he alone did not have the power to defeat Makuta.

Then again, I'm not alone, he thought, looking at the Mask of Time he carried. *If Makuta wants this mask so badly, maybe it's time to let him have it.*

Vakama climbed up the next access ladder he came to and emerged on a Ta-Metru street, near the Protodermis Reclamation Yard. That, he decided, would make a perfect setting for his confrontation with Makuta.

No allies, he told himself. *No Keetongu, no other Toa, just me, Makuta, and this mask. Mata Nui altered the stars themselves to ensure that I would become a Toa — it's time to show the Great Spirit he made the right decision.*

Makuta climbed the ladder slowly. He would never have admitted it to anyone else, but the Shadowed One had wounded him far worse than any other being ever had. His Kanohi mask and armor held his dark energies in place. With his breastplate damaged, precious power was slipping away from him. But there was no time to make repairs, not with Vakama on the loose with the Mask of Time.

He will give it to me willingly, or I will take it from his corpse, Makuta thought. *In fact, I hope the fool tries to fight — it will make my victory that much sweeter. Perhaps I will send his remains to the other Toa Metru so that they may enjoy a few moments of fear before I destroy them, too.*

He looked around, searching for signs of Vakama. He had no doubt the Toa was hiding somewhere nearby, making some feeble plan for an ambush. Perhaps he was even thinking of using the Mask of Time again, not that that would do anything but buy him a couple more minutes of life.

"Show yourself, Toa!" Makuta shouted. "Give me the Mask of Time and I will let you go on your way. I am sure your fellow 'heroes' are missing you by now."

The only answer was silence. In a strange way, that enraged Makuta more than open defiance would have.

"Why do you persist?" the master of shadows continued. "You will gain nothing from this but death, Vakama, here, alone in this ruined city. There will be no one to mourn you here, no one to even notice your passing. You will not die a hero — just a pathetic Matoran playing at a role that was never meant for him. Why do you risk death? Why do you insist on opposing me?"

Vakama stepped out from an alleyway in the Protodermis Reclamation Yard, one hand hidden behind his back. "Because I'm a Toa," he said, his voice strong and clear. "And battling monsters is what I do."

Makuta's smile was chilling. "I, a monster? For knowing my spirit brother, Mata Nui, required a good, long rest after his many labors? For offering my benevolent leadership to the Matoran in his absence? For saving Metru Nui from the threat of Nidhiki and Krekka?"

Vakama saw that Makuta was circling as he spoke, hoping to distract the Toa while he got into a position to strike. But he wasn't dealing with a novice Toa Metru now. "Yes, Makuta," said

Vakama. "The Dark Hunters you brought here, and then murdered . . . just like you murdered Turaga Lhikan . . . and sentenced an entire city to a sleeping doom. Yes, I call you monster — and worse."

Makuta eyed his enemy. Vakama was standing next to a stopped conveyor belt upon which rested a line of damaged Kanohi masks. He was startled to see that the Vahi, intact, was among them. And all that stood between him and one of the most powerful Kanohi masks in creation was one foolish Toa.

"Your words are like your powers, Vakama — fiery, but in the end, meaningless," said the master of shadows. "Now I will take that mask you so jealously guard."

Makuta took a step forward. Vakama took his hand from behind his back, revealing that he held a Ta-Matoran crafter's hammer. With blinding speed, he lashed out and smashed one of the damaged masks to fragments.

"Not just yet," said the Toa. "How much do you know about the Mask of Time? Do you know, for example, that it still works even when damaged? I found that out the day I retrieved it from the ocean floor."

Vakama smashed a damaged Mask of Water Breathing.

"The merest crack and the power of time leaks out of it, affecting everything in the vicinity," the Toa of Fire continued. "Isn't that fascinating?"

He shattered another mask, and then another. There were only two more between his hammer and the Mask of Time.

"Stop this childishness," Makuta hissed. "You wouldn't destroy your greatest creation, maskmaker."

"Yes, I suppose that would be hard to live with," Vakama said, smashing yet another mask. The sound echoed through the empty streets of Ta-Metru. "But, then, if I were to shatter the Mask of Time, neither of us will *be* living, the way we think of living . . . and neither will anyone else."

Makuta watched him carefully, calculating odds. A rapid burst of shadow energy would destroy the hammer, as well as stun Vakama. But if he should miss?

"Explain," he said, edging closer to the Toa.

"Time, Makuta," Vakama replied, as if speaking to a child. "The force of time is contained within that mask. Destroy it, and that power is unleashed upon the universe. Past, present, and future all existing at once — warps and rips and hours folding in upon each other — madness and chaos as no two moments ever follow one another . . . think of it."

"I am," said the armored figure. "It sounds *glorious*."

"Really?" Vakama said, shattering another mask to splinters. "Imagine your body trapped between seconds, or half of you aging while the other half regresses. Does it still sound appealing to you? All your plans and schemes would come to an end, because no matter what you attempted, I could walk into the past and undo it. Kill me today, and I will be waiting for you in some tomorrow to avenge my death."

Vakama's hammer hovered over the Mask of Time, ready to strike. "Think of it — can you rule a future that is in the past? Or a present that is still a century away? Could you ever be sure what you have done and what you haven't, when months and years have merged together?"

Makuta pondered. If Vakama was telling the truth, destroying the Kanohi Vahi would bring the universe to a crashing halt. Still, he could not believe a Toa would willingly visit such a fate upon the Matoran he had sworn to protect.

"Believe it," Vakama said, as if he had read his mind. "To save those I love from an eternity of your tyranny, I will end everything right now."

Makuta looked into Vakama's eyes. They were the eyes of a being who had been driven beyond madness, only to return. They had looked upon a darkness as deep as any Makuta had known, and yet somehow turned back to the light. They were not the eyes of a being who was bluffing.

"What do you want, Toa?" Makuta said finally.

"Safe passage from Metru Nui for myself and this mask," Vakama said. "Your pledge not to harm Keetongu, Turaga Dume, or the Rahaga . . . and to leave the Matoran in peace."

Makuta took two quick steps forward, propelled by anger. It was only the sight of Vakama swinging the hammer that brought him up short. "You ask me to sit in the darkness, doing nothing, affecting nothing!" the master of shadows snapped. "You sentence me to a living death, and I say no! Go ahead, destroy the mask, and we will watch time end together." Vakama began to lower the hammer. "Wait!" Makuta cried. Vakama stopped, his hammer mere inches from the mask.

"Then what is your offer?" the Toa asked calmly. "And make it quick — my arm grows tired."

The armored titan snarled. He was not used to negotiating with lesser beings, but there was one consolation. As long as the Mask of Time existed, it might still be his one day. "Very well," he said. "I will respect your allies here, as long as they stay out of my way. I will even let you leave unharmed. And I will grant you one year of peace on the island above, and one year only. Then . . . you will hear from me again."

Vakama considered. He knew the other Toa would never accept such a deal, simply because they would never believe Makuta would honor it. They would insist on battle, even Nokama, to end his threat here and now . . . despite the fact that such a battle would leave Metru Nui damaged beyond all hope of restoration.

"Do not try my patience," Makuta growled. "Your possession of the Mask of Time may leave me inclined to stay my hand, but we both know there are a thousand ways I could destroy you right now. And 941 of them hurt."

Vakama lowered his hammer and picked up the Mask of Time. "How do I know you'll keep your word?"

Makuta smiled. "You don't. But what is life without a little risk, Toa?"

Vakama was about to reply when the world vanished around him. The next moment, he was standing at the mouth of one of the tunnels that led to the island above. He still had the Mask of Time with him.

Makuta has expelled me from my city, he thought. *But we will make a new home above, master of shadows, one we will defend against you to the death. And one day, when you have finally been defeated, we will return to the City of Legends. This I vow, in the name of all Toa and Matoran!*

Epilogue 1

Makuta stood at the edge of a subterranean waterway. Once, this river had been the means of escape for six Toa Metru and six pods filled with sleeping Matoran. Here they had encountered ancient Rahi sea beasts and done great battle. They had won in the end and made it to the island above.

All of this Makuta had read in Vakama's mind, plus one thing more: Not all the pods had made it to safety. One had been torn loose from the boat by a Rahi and now lay abandoned on the river bottom.

Makuta summoned the power of magnetism to raise the metallic sphere from its watery resting place. It broke the surface and floated in the air before finally coming to rest at the armored feet of the master of shadows.

The pressing of the latch opened the pod. Inside there slept a Po-Matoran named Ahkmou. Makuta smiled at the sight. This Matoran had already attempted to betray the Toa and his home city once before. He would be ideal for what Makuta had in mind.

An infinitesimal fraction of the Dark One's power brought consciousness back to Ahkmou. The Matoran opened his eyes and looked around in panic. "Where am I? How did I get here? What *is* this place?"

Makuta had expected just this sort of reaction. The pods were designed to erase the memories of those inside, making them more easily influenced when they revived. He reached down and helped the Matoran out of the pod. "Yes, little one, your mind is filled with questions now. But I will provide you with answers, and in return, you will do something for me in the time to come."

Together, the master of shadows and the Po-Matoran began a long journey into perpetual darkness.

"Let me tell you a tale," said Makuta as they walked. "A tale of a city called Metru Nui and of a band of beings called Toa who conspired to keep greatness from you and then abandoned you to spend eternity at the bottom of this river. They feared you, as they do me, but now I have rescued you. Together, we will seek justice against them for their crimes."

Ahkmou nodded. He did not remember how he had gotten into the pod or ended up in this awful place. But there was no question this heroic figure had saved his life. As he listened to the intricate web of lies spun by Makuta, Ahkmou vowed that one day he would have revenge on Toa, Turaga, and Matoran, wherever they might hide.

Epilogue 2

Turaga Vakama heard the hum of excitement throughout the boat as the shoreline came into sight. He allowed himself a moment's satisfaction, knowing that he had fulfilled his vow to someday return.

After leaving Metru Nui for the last time, he had made his way back to the island above. He told the other Toa that he had successfully found the Mask of Time, along with evidence that proved they had been meant to be Toa Metru all along. About the events he had witnessed and been part of in the city, he said nothing. The knowledge that Makuta waited down below might have spurred them to attack, and a war at that point would have left the Matoran in dire jeopardy.

Makuta was as good as his word. One year to the day after the Toa Metru woke the Matoran, he unleashed Rahi attacks on their new villages. It was a frightening time, but Vakama knew that if Makuta had wanted to destroy the Matoran, he could have easily done so. No, he was trying to keep them off balance, afraid, and as far away from Metru Nui as possible.

It took more than one thousand years and an entirely new team of Toa, but Makuta's plans had been undone. The master of shadows had fallen to the power of light, and the way was open for the Matoran to return to their homeland. The first step had been taken toward awakening the Great Spirit Mata Nui and restoring balance to the universe.

Ta-Matoran leaped out of the boat and pulled it the last few yards to the bank, while other crews did the same all around them. Turaga Dume and the six Rahaga were already rushing down to greet the new arrivals. Vakama could not suppress a smile as he set foot in Metru Nui for the first time in over a millennium.

Time Trap

The City of Legends belonged to the Matoran once more. And no one, Vakama vowed — not the Dark Hunters, not the Brotherhood of Makuta, nor anyone else — would ever take it from them again.

As past, present, and possibly even future Toa met on the shore, Vakama stood apart and watched. He could not help but wish Toa Lhikan had been there to witness this moment. Still, even if that great hero was not present physically, Vakama had no doubt his spirit was watching over them all.

"Turaga Vakama?"

Vakama turned to see Hahli, the Chronicler, approaching. "Yes, little one?"

"Do you have any more tales to tell of the past?"

Vakama smiled and shook his head. "There will always be new tales to be written and new tales to be shared. But it is time to stop speaking of the past, Hahli — we have a future to build, together."